PANZER HUNT

Leo Kessler

Panzer Hunt

Futura Publications Limited

A Futura Book

First published in Great Britain by
Futura Publications Limited in 1979

Copyright © Futura Publications 1979

ISBN 0 7088 1520 0
Printed by
William Collins Sons & Co. Ltd
Glasgow

Futura Publications Limited,
110 Warner Road, Camberwell,
London SE5

To The Waffen SS

Proudly they marched
With youthful arrogance and voices raised in song
True to their insignia and to allegiance sworn,
For they were born
The Chosen, the Elite, the cream of Deutschland's sons,
Far beyond the call of duty to excel
Unflinching where lesser breeds would fear to tread;
Unyielding they pressed on or fell.

Invincible they were;
No mortal foe could stem their forward surge,
Only the blinding snow sweeping a desolate waste
Could seal their fate.
In all their splendid youth,
Defying even Nature's cruel bitter mood,
Side by side in comradeship, hand helping hand,
They suffered and endured.

Do not weep for them,
Those who fell with faith in their ideals,
For Wotan's daughters swept them up on fiery steeds
And for immortal deeds
In Valhalla they live on.
They would find no part in our world of ebbing tide,
Where discipline and honour are just words
To mock and deride.

Fight on survivors!
Raise your voices high above the storm!
Many will support you and also wish to serve,
For those who fell deserve
A memory unblemished, undefiled,
Their glory echoing down the years to sons and sons of sons.
The time is coming when a world no longer sane
Must once again be purified
So from obscurity and dust and ashes
Stand ready for the day to rise again . . .

Eddi Glastra, Spring 1978

One: The Last Battle

'The war's over . . . We're gonna live like God in France!'
Trooper Matz,   June 1940

ONE

Swaying back and forth in the turret of the armoured reconnaissance car, Captain von Dodenburg fought to control his drowsiness. Through half-closed eyes, his face lathered with sweat in the heat of the June afternoon, he barely perceived the tall poplars that swept by on both sides of the interminable, cobbled French road as the armoured car rolled steadily southwards.

Ever since *SS Assault Battalion Wotan* had captured Fort Eben Emael the previous month,* the survivors of that élite regiment, hurriedly reinforced by eager volunteers from the *Reich*, had been driving through France, herding the shattered French armies before them. Hour after hour, day after day, week after week, they had rolled on through the smouldering French countryside. Everywhere there had been the flutter of white – the white of surrender. Flags, tablecloths, bedsheets, towels: every house, farm, church steeple and cottage bore the symbol of France's defeat.

Here and there, the weary, demoralized *poilus* turned and tried to put up a token defence. But Wotan's tanks swept the hastily improvised French barricades aside as if they were made of matchwood. Their impatient commander, The Vulture, urged them on with his high-pitched, almost feverish cries.

'Tempo . . . *tempo*! Smash the Frogs! If Wotan's the first German unit to reach the sea, it'll mean the laurel leaves to my tin. *Tempo, you death-dogs!*' †

---

* See *SS Panzer Battalion* for further details.
† The coveted 'laurel leaves' to add to the Knight's Cross of the Iron Cross, which he had already won at Fort Eben Emael.

Lyon, Vienne, Valence, Montelimar, Orange – they had all come and gone in Wotan's hectic dash for the port of Nîmes and the Mediterranean. Now, finally, they were approaching the last known French line of defence in the foothills that surrounded the port. In spite of the fact that he knew he was riding point, the blond, harshly handsome *SS* captain could not keep his eyes open. The heat, the fatigue of these last, hectic weeks and the emptiness of the lush southern French countryside lulled him into an uneasy doze. Captain von Dodenburg did not even notice the sudden funnel of black smoke that started to rise into the deep blue sky immediately the lone armoured car had passed the first hidden look-out.

They rolled on, radio chattering incessantly as the operator reported back to an impatient Vulture with the tanks, the driver taking each new bend with fearsome care, only to speed up again when he discovered that the vineyards on both sides of the cobbled road were empty once more. Captain von Dodenburg started to snore heavily.

Crump!

The first shell fell just short of the armoured car. Red-hot shell splinters beat a drum-roll on the steel glacis plate. The windshield shattered. Desperately, the driver clung to the wheel, suddenly blinded, his face bleeding from a myriad cuts.

'What in three devils' name?' Captain von Dodenburg gasped, wrenching his eyes open in alarm.

The hidden 75 mm fired again. The still air was ripped apart. The front off-side tyre burst. The driver tried desperately to hold the eight-ton vehicle – and failed. Metal howling under the strain, rubber squealing, the armoured car careened right across the road and smashed into the ditch. The point of *SS Assault Battalion Wotan* had run right into the French trap!

For one long moment, Captain von Dodenburg lay there in the crazy jumble of the turret, listening to the still-running motor. Then he remembered where he was. 'Driver?' he gasped, wiping the blood from his nostrils.

'Gone for a hop, sir,' the radio operator breathed, pulling himself free from the earphones. 'Better make dust before the Frogs start coming to look for us, eh?'

'Yes, bale out – at the double!' von Dodenburg ordered urgently. Freeing his machine-pistol, he pulled himself over the side of the turret.

In that same instant the heavy silence was shattered by the hysterical scream of a high-power enemy machine-gun. Lead plucked at his tousled blond hair as it hissed by and ripped a line of holes in the bank behind him. He ducked. Instinctively he pressed the trigger of his Schmeisser, spraying bullets across the vineyard to his right. 'Operator,' he bellowed, 'bring the portable – I'll cover you!'

He dropped to the ground, crouched like a western gun-fighter and covered the radio operator, who flung himself over the side, clutching the portable radio to his chest like a loving mother carrying her baby.

Together, lead slicing the air all around them and stitching patterns in the dust at their flying heels, they raced for the opposite ditch and flung themselves into it, just as the hidden 75 mm opened up again, buffeting their pale, excited faces with its blast. Captain von Dodenburg opened his mouth instinctively, knowing that this was the only way to save his eardrums; he felt his lungs fill with the acrid, choking smell of cordite and gasped, 'Operator, take a message for the CO.'

'Sir?' the radio operator bellowed over the shriek of yet another 75 mm shell.

'Report our position and tell him that – ' the howl of another incoming shell drowned his words momentarily ' – that we've been caught with our knickers down. The Frogs have got us by the short and curlies.'

Von Dodenburg brought up his machine-pistol, while the radio operator bent over his apparatus, his face suddenly full of apprehension. Figures in dark-blue uniform had risen everywhere amongst the vines and were beginning to walk towards the wrecked armoured car in a steady, thoughtful manner. The French were coming in for the kill. The captain grasped the black and white enamel of his Knight's

Cross at the throat of his black leather jacket and prepared to battle for his life.

The Vulture tugged at the monstrous beak of a nose which had given him his nickname in *SS Assault Battalion Wotan*, and waited impatiently while his radio operator scribbled down the message he was presently receiving. All around, the half-naked tankers sprawled in the turrets of their Mark IIIs, sleeping or talking in the tones of men who had been pushed too hard. Finally he could stand the waiting no longer. Slapping his cane against the side of the baggy, outsize grey breeches which marked him as regular cavalry-man, he barked in his high-pitched nasal voice, 'Well, out with it, man. What has Captain von Dodenburg to report?'

The operator paused in the middle of his scribbling, sweat running down his hairless chest, which The Vulture noted with some slight pleasure was still a delicate and very pleasing white in spite of the burning June sun. 'Sir, Captain von Dodenburg says he has bumped into the French line. His armoured car has been wrecked and he's surrounded by French infantry.'

'Position?' The Vulture barked.

The operator gave him it and added, 'And what about Captain von Dodenburg, sir? What should I tell him?'

The Vulture paused in mid-stride. 'Tell him to look after himself as best he can. I have other things to do,' he snapped, his ice-blue, ruthless eyes already gleaming with excitement and anticipation at the knowledge of the whereabouts of the French position. 'Metzger! Sergeant Metzger!' he bellowed at the big bull of a battalion sergeant-major. 'Get Companies Two and Three on the move! Captain von Dodenburg's One will stay in reserve. Come on, man, get the lead out of your boots!'

'At your command, sir!' Metzger bellowed back, his broad, ugly face brick-red. 'All right, you bunch of garden dwarfs, you heard the Major.' He took up his favourite pose in front of the suddenly alert tank crews, boots wide apart, chest and apelike jaw thrust out, beefy butcher's hands on

12

his hips. It was a position he had once seen in an old film about the Kaiser's army and he had practised it secretly in front of the mirror in his quarters until he had made it perfect. 'Two and Three, hands off yer cocks and on with yer socks. *Mount up!*'

Engine after engine burst into an ear-splitting cacophony. Suddenly the air was thick with choking blue fumes. Tracks clanking, showering those who were going to remain behind with pebbles and earth, the first Mark III moved off to do battle. *SS Assault Battalion Wotan's* last fight in France had begun.

TWO

'She was really something special, Matzi, something special. I'll lay odds a good many men would go to war on her behalf – if they had any energy left!'

SS Trooper Matz looked up from his task – cleaning his toe-nails with the tip of his bayonet – and stared scornfully at his big companion, Corporal Schulze, who was busy running a lighted cigarette along the seams of his shirt to drive out the lice. 'Since when have you liked girls, you big, soft warm brother? The only love juice you've ever – ' He stopped suddenly. A dark shadow had fallen between the two running-mates. 'Don't look now, Schulze,' he continued, 'but I think we are being observed.'

'I think you're right, Matzi,' Schulze answered easily. He raised his huge right buttock and gave one of his celebrated farts. 'Heil Hitler, Sergeant-Major!'

Metzger, or The Butcher, as he was known throughout Wotan, smiled down maliciously at the two half-naked men relaxing in the grass. 'One day, Schulze, that big trap of yours is gonna get yer in trouble. Risk a fat lip like that with a Gestapo man around and you're right on yer way to the big smoke.' His forefinger, as thick as any sausage he had ever made in his days behind the meat counter, circled upwards to indicate the smoke emerging from a concentration camp oven.

Schulze grabbed the front of his grey pants and simpered 'Oh, please Mr Sergeant-Major, don't say things like that. You'll have me peeing in my pants with fear. You know how fragile and delicate I am, you naughty man!'

'Like hell!' The Butcher growled, his face brick-red.

14

'Oh, isn't he so coarse, Schulzi darling,' Matz said with a flip of a limp hand. 'We girls from the convent aren't used to that kind of language.'

Sergeant-Major Metzger ignored the leather-faced runt of an SS man. 'Listen,' he said, enjoying himself, 'I've got something to tell you two.'

Schulze pouted seductively. 'Give us a kiss first, Sergeant-Major.'

The Butcher did not allow himself to be deflected. 'You heard Companies Two and Three move out just now, didn't you? Well, do you know why your shower didn't go off with them to have a crack at the shitting Frogs?'

'No,' Schulze said, his flippant mood gone now, aware that The Butcher would not have exerted himself in the June heat to come over to the Number One Company lines for nothing. 'But you're gonna tell us in a minute. So, pull your digit out of your awful orifice and cough it up.'

'Have some respect for rank – ' The Butcher began, then caught himself in time. 'Your CO – Captain von Dodenburg – has gone and landed himself right in the shit now,' he continued, uttering the words in pleasurable anticipation of the reaction to come. He got it.

'What did you say?' Schulze barked, iron in his voice now.

'Put a "sir" on that question.'

'What's happened to the CO – *sir*? And don't kid me, Metzger, or you'll be lacking a set of choppers.' As if by magic, a gleaming set of brass knuckles had appeared, wrapped firmly round his right fist. 'Remember, Metzger, the Hamburger Equalizer,' he indicated the brass knuckles, 'don't care whether you're a sergeant-major or not. Now spit it out.'

The Butcher drew a deep breath and looked at the big ex-Hamburg docker's angry face, then at his fist. In that instant, he decided he would not stand on his rank. Schulze would not hesitate one moment; he would smash anybody from Skorzeny down to get his information, come what may. 'Well, it's like this . . .' he began.

When he had finished, Matz stared at him increduously and whispered, 'And you mean that that little arsehole of a

Vulture isn't gonna do anything to help the CO?'

Metzger shook his head pleasurably, knowing just how much the two suddenly pale soldiers admired their company commander. 'No,' he said, 'he has other things to do. Captain von Dodenburg will have to look after himself for the time being. The attack on the Frog line comes first.'

'Would you believe it!' Matz exploded. 'The CO has been riding at point for days now, sticking his neck out time and time again so the bleeding Vulture can win some more tin and a fresh promotion, and the first time the Captain gets into trouble – '

He stopped short. Schulze was not listening. 'You gone crazy or something?' he asked, puzzled. 'Now what?'

Schulze shook his head, as if he were suddenly waking up from a deep sleep. 'Now what, you Aryan idiot!' he bellowed. 'I'll tell you what.' He grabbed for his shirt and struggled into it, lice falling from the seams like grey snow. 'We're gonna carve the CO out of the mess he's gotten himself into. Start up that glorified tin box on wheels.'

'Hey!' The Butcher protested, as Matz started pelting to his Mark III. 'You can't run off with a tank just like that, without permission. If – '

He never finished. Schulze gave him one shove with a hand like a small battering ram and sent him sprawling. Next moment the huge corporal was running after his companion.

The little hamlet stank of dead bodies, smoke and burning sugar from the factory at its edge. It was now well ablaze after the three swift rounds that Schulze had sent zapping through its thin brick walls. The big Hamburger, well protected in the Mark III's glowing turret, swung his periscope from side to side, surveying the first barrier on the road to rescuing his CO. The French were firing from behind barricades made of the bodies of their dead comrades. Behind them, a handful of soldiers were trying to build a barricade out of farmcarts and a couple of rolls of rusty barbed wire. He sniffed contemptuously. 'One good fart,

Matzi,' he announced, 'and I'd blow the whole bloody lot to Kingdom Come. All right, short-ass, roll 'em!'

Matz shoved home first gear and let out the clutch. The 420 hp Maibach engine roared. With a lurch, the Mark III started to roll ever closer towards the French positions.

A single ancient machine-gun covered the bridge they would have to cross. Almost carelessly, Schulze pressed the trigger of his high-power co-axial turret machine-gun. The loader clutched his chest, stitched a sudden ghastly red, and fell flat on his face across the blood-stained cobbles. Another soldier ran out of the shelter of an arch to take his place. Schulze let off another swift burst ripping him in two, catapulting the twin halves of his body over the bank and into the river below.

'Jesus, Schulze!' Matz breathed over the intercom in undisguised admiration, 'some great shooting!'

'You ain't seen nothing yet,' Schulze said. 'Focus your glassy orbs on this one.'

Taking careful aim at the gunner who lay flat on the cobbles, body twisted at the prescribed forty-five degree angle so that he presented a damnably difficult target to hit, he fired a burst. The 9 mm slugs howled off the cobbles ten metres away from the French gunner in a flurry of blue sparks. Exactly as Schulze had planned it, they struck the gunner directly in the face. It disappeared in a mess of gore through which peered two empty eye sockets. The gunner went down screaming and writhing in pain. One moment later the Mark III rolled over his body, squashing it as flat as a cardboard cut-out. The tank shuddered and drove on, one limp arm jerking up and down in its tracks, as if waving a mocking goodbye to the dead French soldiers that lay around it. An instant later the Mark III had crashed through the pathetic barricade and disappeared down the road towards the next enemy position.

THREE

Von Dodenburg had a momentary, terrifying glimpse of blinding light. An instant later it was followed by two blazing rings of violent colour. His head was jerked back by a heavy blow on the helmet. He felt an excruciating pain in his ears. He shook his head and tried to focus his eyes on the shattered body of the radio operator, which lay at his feet, now minus his head. He failed.

'What – ' he gasped to no one in particular, as the cannon erupted once more. A blinding shower of rubble, dirt and pebbles thrashed his face. He fought desperately for breath, like a drowning man. He felt himself being blown from the wrecked armoured car. He tried to grab a hold somewhere. There was none. Twice he tried to fight the blast and rise. To no avail.

The 75 mm fired again. This time it ripped the Schmeisser out of his nerveless fingers, and he was blown even further from the protection of the vehicle. Blood poured down his face. The whole world was ablaze with colour, and a loud crazy ringing sounded in his ears. Somehow he staggered to his feet, crying, 'Stop . . . stop, for God's sake, or I'll go crazy! Do you hear – '

Captain von Dodenburg stopped short. A tall, menacing figure loomed up out of the haze in front of his eyes – a man carrying a long, old-fashioned rifle that did not belong to the German Army in his bony, reddened fingers. He jerked the muzzle in the German's direction and mumbled something that von Dodenburg did not understand. But the gesture was clear enough. Slowly, groggily, Captain von Dodenburg began to raise his bleeding hands.

Holding their rifles fixed on him, their dirt-streaked faces greased with sweat, the French soldiers stood round their captive, as if they were wondering what to do with him next. For a few moments the alarming thought shot through von Dodenburg's mind that they were going to finish him off there and then. In the heat of battle, and especially in the mood the French must be now, soldiers found a quick bullet in the back of the head was the easiest way of getting rid of the burden of a prisoner.

Von Dodenburg glared at them as haughtily as he could manage, trying to make them feel uncomfortable, even guilty, for having captured *him*, an officer of the élite *SS Assault Battalion Wotan*.

'You're *SS*, aren't you?' one of the Frenchmen asked in the accent of the Alsace.

Von Dodenburg turned to look at the man, a heavily built, blond giant with the stripes of a sergeant on his cuff. 'Yes,' he admitted.

The Alsatian pulled a face. 'That's not good,' he said.

'What do you mean?' von Dodenburg asked.

The man shrugged a little helplessly. 'I'm from the border with Germany myself. I know the difference between the Armed *SS* and those turds who guard the concentration camps. But this lot – ' Again he shrugged.

'So?' von Dodenburg prompted.

'So, they'll shoot you – sooner or later,' the Alsatian answered after an awkward pause. 'All right,' he jerked his rifle at von Dodenburg. 'We'll get back for interrogation, and then – '

He left the rest of the sentence unsaid, as if he did not feel it wise to put his thoughts into words.

Hands raised above his head, Captain von Dodenburg

stumbled forward, hardly able to believe that in an hour or two he would be lying crumpled at the base of some bullet-pocked farmyard wall.

'Well?' Matz demanded impatiently.

Slowly Schulze lowered his binoculars and then dropped off the top of the haystack where he had observed the little scene taking place half a kilometre away. 'They've got him – the CO.'

'Heaven, arse and cloudburst,' Matz cursed and punched his fist at the steel flank of the concealed Mark III. 'What bloody tough luck!'

'Don't worry, Matzi. Those poor Frog banana-suckers don't know what they've let themselves in for when they've got Captain von Dodenburg as a prisoner.'

'I hope you're right, Schulze,' Matz said without too much confidence. 'You know what blokes are – '

'Of course I'm right.' Schulze cut him short, putting more confidence in his voice than he felt. After all, he had seen the looks on the enemy faces. He knew what they meant. 'Come on, Matzi, get the lead out of your boots. Let's get the show on the road!'

FOUR

It was nearly dark now. Angry red lights glowed on the horizon like the flames from an enormous blast furnace. The earth trembled beneath the waiting men's feet.

The Vulture lowered his binoculars. The artillery was doing a good job. It was time to take in Companies Two and Three. 'Signal pistol,' he rasped to the waiting aide.

The pale-faced young second lieutenant, a reinforcement, who, The Vulture thought privately, was a very pretty boy indeed, handed him the bell-shaped pistol swiftly.

The Vulture did not hesitate. He raised it above his head and pulled both triggers. The twin green flares soared into the air. With a soft plop they exploded, bathing the faces of the waiting infantry a sickly green, before they started to tumble down across the sky like fallen angels.

The tankers on both flanks reacted immediately. Bursting out from their hiding places in haystacks, barns and farm-yards, they began to clatter towards the French line. The Vulture nodded his head in appreciation, and raising his cane, his only weapon, he cried in his strangely high-pitched voice: 'Grenadiers – *grenadiers, advance!*'

'At the double!' the NCOs cried.

'Come on now, let's be having you,' the officers ordered.

'*Alles fuer Deutschland!*'* The hoarse cry rose from half a hundred young throats.

The Vulture beamed. The raw recruits were eager for a hero's death. 'After me, you dogs,' he cried. 'You don't want to live for ever, do you!' He turned to the handsome young

---

* 'Everything for Germany,' the battle-cry of the Armed SS.

aide and felt a thrill of anticipation as he did so. 'Come on, young man, this day you'll earn your pay!'

In a ragged line, flanked on both sides by the lumbering steel monsters, the men of the *SS Assault Battalion Wotan* ran towards the enemy.

The leading NCO skidded to a halt. He dropped to his knee, shoulders tensed. The blond giant behind him reacted instinctively, just as he had been trained to do. He thrust the air-cooled barrel of the Spandau across the NCO's right shoulder and pressed the trigger. At a rate of eight hundred rounds a minute, the vicious red and white tracer hissed straight up the cobbled road into the barn where the first French position was located. Wood splintered. Abruptly, the front of the barn was riddled with smoking holes.

The Vulture ran up, gasping for breath. Viciously he slashed his riding crop across the blond giant's shoulders. 'Aim at the window, you oaf. The *window*, or I'll have the eggs off you with a blunt razor blade!'

The giant took a more careful aim. The heavy, air-cooled machine-gun bounced up and down on the NCO's shoulders. The window shattered. The French soldier who had been firing from it screamed shrilly and tumbled out to hit the cobbles below like a sack of wet cement.

'*Forward!*' The Vulture ordered, now that obstacle had been overcome. '*Forward*, I say, you hounds of hell!' He lay about them with his cane, slashing the reluctant young grenadiers' backs. Raw and inexperienced as they were, they were more scared of The Vulture than the enemy. They rose and dashed into the attack once more. The Vulture beamed and sprang over the writhing body of one of his men.

The attack was going well.

'Comrades, help me,' a grenadier screamed pitifully, his face a red, eyeless mess. 'I'm blinded . . . blinded.' He

22

staggered forward, directly into the French crossfire which had caught the charging grenadiers completely by surprise. He was dead before he had gone five metres.

Now the crossfire poured into his trapped, frightened and sweating companions.

The Vulture saw the danger immediately. 'Stand fast, damn your eyes! *Stand fast!*' he bellowed, standing upright himself, totally ignoring the hail of lead whizzing past him. A panicked farm-horse clattered by, foam bubbling from slack lips, its mane flying behind. A second later it went down on his forelegs, whinnying hysterically, as it took the burst intended for the little officer.

The Vulture did not even notice. His glass-clear eyes were trying to ascertain the tactical situation. He knew he had only a matter of moments to make up his mind and act; if he failed, his raw recruits would panic, throw away their weapons and run for it. He must get his men out of that murderous crossfire. His tanks, positioned as they were on both flanks, were of no use. They could not help him among the houses; they would be an easy target for the French grenade-throwers.

'NCOs,' he commanded, 'get your men into the houses on both sides of the street. At the double! Break into the houses!'

The NCOs needed no urging. Blowing their whistles and bellowing orders, they charged with the grenadiers, springing over the bodies of their dead and dying comrades. At once they started to break into the French cottages, smashing in windows and doors with the butts of their rifles, taking murderous numbers of casualties all the time as the hidden French machine-gunners directed their fire at the bunched troopers. Then they were in, fighting and clawing at each other to get away from that hellish fire, leaving the dead piled up in great heaps on the road outside.

The Vulture thrust back his peaked cap – he never wore a helmet – and breathed out a sigh of relief. For the time being he had prevented a panic. But for how long? The French would counter-attack soon and if they used flame-throwers, which they often did for street-fighting, he wondered how long he would be able to hold the rabble of frightened, wide-eyed boys who cowered all around him, starting violently every time a fresh burst of machine-gun fire racked the wall.

FIVE

The French major, dark-faced and unshaven but resolute, every inch a soldier, stared up at von Dodenburg in the light of the flickering candle, which shook violently every time the 75 mm cannon in the yard outside fired. 'You are of the *SS*, Captain?' he snapped in good German.

Von Dodenburg nodded. There was no use trying to deny the fact; the silver *SS* runes on his collar and his death's head cap badge told the full story.

'You understand the gravity of your position, Captain?'

'What do you mean, Major?'

The expression on the French soldier's face did not change; it remained as hard and unyielding as before, and there was no emotion in his voice when he answered. 'We have orders to shoot any of the *SS* who fall into our hands. At last our High Command has found some spine. It has begun to make decisions – hard decisions.'

Captain von Dodenburg bit his bottom lip. 'But surely you can't risk shooting me for doing my job as a soldier – not now, Major, not when France has already lost the war. You might well be facing a German superior in a few days' time, just as I am facing you at this moment. How will you account for your actions? *You* would be the war criminal, and I'm sure you know the punishment for that.'

The French Major nodded calmly, completely unmoved. 'Naturally. But you must understand; if we have lost the war, as you say, France will need victims – heroes, if you like – to justify that defeat.' He shrugged and waited till the candle stopped its wild flickering, as the 75 mm erupted once again. 'If I cannot die for France on the battlefield, I will certainly be prepared to do so in front of a German firing squad.'

He barked an order in French. The Alsatian unshouldered his rifle and took von Dodenburg by the arm. 'Come,' he said gently. 'You must come with me.'

'But what are you going to do with me?' von Dodenburg asked, hardly able to believe that this was happening to him – not *now*, not after all the dangers of the long campaign had been overcome and the end was in sight. The French major did not look up from the map he had begun to study and it was left to the Alsatian to inform von Dodenburg of his fate as they stepped out into the debris-littered farmyard. Dust-covered despatch-riders were skidding to a halt or roaring away with fresh orders in their leather pouches, and a long line of wounded and bleeding men waited to be treated at the dressing station. 'I'm sorry, Captain,' he said, 'but the Major has ordered you to be shot.'

'When?' von Dodenburg asked through lips which had gone suddenly dry.

The Alsatian looked at the ground, shifting from one foot to the other.

'At dawn,' he answered.

'Gimme your flatman,' Schulze ordered, wiping the sweat from his broad brow.

'I suppose you think your God's bleeding gift, don't yer,' Matz replied and applied the brakes.

'Natch. Didn't yer know? I walk over the water every Friday as well. Give!' He stretched down a huge paw and Matz dutifully passed up the nearly empty bottle of schnapps.

Schulze unscrewed the cap and drained it. Then he belched and tossed the empty bottle out of the turret.

'What – another dead soldier?' Matz cried. 'Where do you put that stuff? That's my second flatman you've emptied tonight.'

'Got holler legs, that's what I've got,' Schulze growled. 'Now tie a knot in yer skinny neck and shut up. I've got to think.'

'Yes, Mr Corporal,' Matz answered with mock humility. 'Would this Mr Corporal like me to powder his hairy arse or hold his lily-white hand?'

Schulze muttered an obscenity and concentrated on the problem.

They had seen the CO being escorted by his guards into the farmyard HQ below and after a while brought out again to be placed in what looked like a barn. But then the light had gone altogether and they had been unable to make out how he was being guarded. The general set-up of the French Headquarters, the noise of motor-cycles and staff cars coming and going, plus the persistent thud of the 75 mm cannon, told Schulze that the HQ was heavily occupied. It was going to be a tough nut to crack. For a moment he told himself angrily that The Vulture and his two companies from *Wotan* should have broken through the Frog line long ago.

'It's no use expecting any help from The Vulture.' Matz broke the heavy silence, seemingly reading his running-mate's mind. He indicated the silent pink flashes which lit up the horizon. 'The Battalion's having a rough time of it. *Wotan*'s not going to break through this night. I bet the Old Man'll call up the flyboys at dawn to plaster the Frogs before he attacks again. He's nuts about more tin, but he knows there'll be none for him if he burns up the whole battalion.'

Schulze nodded gloomily. 'Spect you're right, Matzi. But we can't wait till dawn. God knows what the Frogs'll do to him, once they know they're beaten. I don't trust those perverted banana-suckers.'

'You mean – '

'I do.' Schulze cut him short, as if he could not bear to have the dire thought spoken aloud. 'At all events, I'm not gonna to risk it. We've got to go in and carve him out tonight.'

'But how, Schulze? They'll hear us a kilometre away with this thing.' He slapped the metal side of the Mark III almost angrily. 'And besides, in the darkness we're easy meat for them in a tank.'

'I know,' Schulze answered, a note of sudden determination in his voice. 'So we abandon this sledge.'

'What did you say?'

'You heard me, or have you gone deaf again? We go in on foot.'

'Jesus H, Schulze!' Matz said in alarm. 'Haven't you got all yer cups in yer cupboard? If we abandon it and The Vulture finds out, he'll have the nuts off us. We'll be in Torgau* till hell freezes over.'

'Yer, so I suppose,' Schulze said, reaching for his machine-pistol. 'But The Vulture ain't gonna know, is he? Now come on, before you mess your dice-beakers. Let's make dust.'

Dutifully Matz seized his machine-pistol, too, and dropped over the side of the Mark III. A moment later the darkness had swallowed them up.

It was a cool night for June. All the same, von Dodenburg was lathered in sweat, his shirt, black with perspiration, sticking unpleasantly to his muscular back. But he worked on, ignoring the pain in his hands and the sting of the sweat in his eyes. Time was running out fast. There were only three hours to dawn and he had to be out by then. The French major had been too much of a Regular Army man to have been joking with him. The French would shoot him all right; there was no doubt about that.

Grimly, the sweat still dripping from his forehead and lodging in his eyebrows in great opaque pearls, the Captain dug into the hard wood of the barn walls. He worked with the sharpened steel heel-plate from his left boot, which had taken him an hour to loosen.

Time passed swiftly. Twice he heard the latch lifted outside; just in time he was able to fling himself down and feign sleep as the guard checked everything. Now von Dodenburg worked on, digging ever deeper into the wooden joint between two roughly hewn beams, knowing this would be the weakest point in the wall. By now all the nails on his right hand had been splintered and the blood was pouring

* A notorious military prison.

down his burning fingers. He could not afford to let up. He worked on, biting his bottom lip to quell the pain, yet he could not repress the gasps of sheer agony every time his bleeding fingertips caught against the rough edge of the wood.

Then tragedy struck. The thin steel plate snapped and abruptly he was left with a minute bit of jagged steel to carry on with. At that moment he could have broken down and cried. All that work for nothing! He cursed fluently to himself for several minutes, then, pulling off his right jackboot, he began attempting to lever off the one remaining heel-plate with the scrap of steel.

It was two hours to dawn.

'Nigger sweat,' Matz whispered, as they crouched in the bushes fifty metres away from the squat black silhouette of the farm. 'They're brewing up the nigger sweat for their Frog breakfast – over to the right.'

'Trust a short-arsed chowhound like you to be interested in feeding his face when we're out to find the CO.'

'But don't you see, bird-brain,' Matz protested. 'In every army, they allus put the goulash cannons next to the guard room. If they've got the Captain in their calaboose, it's got to be next to the cooks' place. So all we've got to do is to follow that smell of nigger-sweat cooking and it'll probably lead us to their jail. Or would the Mister Corporal like me to walk up to the nearest Frog and ask him to tell me where the nick is?'

'No, the Mister Corporal would like you to put your dong up your own ass and give yourself a cheap thrill,' Schulze retorted scornfully. But he could see Matz's point. There were only two of them and he could guess there were at least a hundred French soldiers in the HQ. They had to get to the CO right away, without blundering about all over the place, carve him out as swiftly and as silently as possible and be on their way before the Frogs knew what had hit them. 'Now listen, Matzi,' he whispered urgently. 'I'm going in first, following that coffee smell. You'll bring up the rear at twenty metres. We want no trouble – there are too many of them. If you bump into any one of them, shaft him without any noise. Use the pistol only as a last resort. Clear?'

'Clear.' As if by magic, a wicked-looking, long-bladed knife appeared in the little man's free hand. 'Well, don't stand there like a fart in a trance, Schulze, running off at the mouth. It'll be light in another hour. Move it, you slack-assed sod.'

Schulze moved it. Schmeisser clutched in his left hand, the Hamburger Equalizer now adorning his right, he slipped out of the trees and into the farmyard.

The last phase of the rescue operation had begun.

SIX

'Hello, this is Sunray . . . Hello, this is Sunray,' The Vulture
rasped into the mike in his high-pitched voice, while outside
the French cannon thudded over and over again, shaking
the miserable little house in which they sheltered so that it
seemed it might fall apart at any moment. 'Do you read me,
Big Friend? Do you read me? Over!'

He pressed the earphones closer to his shaven head with
both hands and tried to drown out the murderous racket
from outside. But all he heard was the frustrating scrabble
of morse and static. 'Big Friend' – the Commander of the
Third Stuka Wing – was obviously not receiving him.

Angrily, he tore off the sweat-soaked earphones and
handed them to the ashen-faced radio operator. 'Keep on
trying, Corporal,' he commanded. 'We need air support. If
we don't get the Stukas by dawn, tell those base stallions of
the Air Force, *SS Assault Battalion Wotan* will no longer
exist. Now get on with it.'

Seizing his stick and slashing a path free for himself
through the cowering, terrified youngsters, some of them
still bleeding badly from splinter wounds, he pressed his
eye to the shell hole in the wall and peered out.

It was still dark. But already the sky, split repeatedly by
the ugly scarlet flashes of the French 75s, was beginning to
turn an ugly grey. Dawn was not far off. The Vulture
twisted his head to one side, ignoring the spent slugs and
fist-sized pieces of red-hot, glowing shell shrapnel which
careened off the houses to clatter on to the corpse-littered
cobbles like heavy tropical rain.

At the far end of the street, in which the surviving grenadiers were trapped, he could make out the dark silhouettes of helmeted men. French infantry. They were obviously massing for a pre-dawn attack. Give them another fifteen minutes and they would come charging in, knowing that their own artillery had pounded the Germans long enough.

Suddenly The Vulture caught his breath. One of the soldiers had a frighteningly familiar pack on his shoulders – and by the scarlet flash of the French cannon, The Vulture could make out what looked like a piece of rubber hose in the man's hand. The worst had come. The man was carrying a flame-thrower. *The French were going to burn them out!*

The Vulture was no coward. Despite his overweening ambition to win decorations and gain promotion, the skinny little major was brave, always at the head of his men in battle. But at that moment the thought of being consumed by that terrible flame made his body tremble. He had seen the horrifying mutilations caused by flame-throwers – hideous lumps of scarred, brilliant-pink flesh that had once been men, hidden away in remote military hospitals, pushed around by the nurses in little wickerwork chairs on wheels. 'Basket cases', the doctors called them. No, he could not stand that. Better death than a living hell.

By an effort of will, The Vulture forced himself to act. 'Operator,' he called, 'have you raised Big Friend yet, damn you?'

The sweating operator raised his head from the glowing set. 'No, sir,' he answered miserably.

'Keep at it!' The Vulture rasped, his voice almost under control once more. 'Give me your rifle,' he commanded the ashen-faced, bleeding grenadier crouching next to him at the wall, and when the man was not quick enough, he pulled the weapon from him and thrust its muzzle through the shell-hole. At the end of the street, the French infantry were splitting into two groups. They were going to attack along both sides of the road. His gaze sought the flame-thrower operator. He cursed. Knowing how vulnerable such men were, the French commander had given the unarmed operator two bodyguards, infantrymen armed with machine-pistols, who had positioned themselves on both sides. All

32

the same, he knew he must attempt to knock the man out before he could use his terrible weapon. Pressing himself close to the hole, he took aim, trying to get a clear shot at the operator.

Twice he thought he had him, but in both instances one of the bodyguards moved in front of the operator just as he was about to press the trigger. The Vulture cursed and wiped his face free of sweat, feeling every nerve in his body tingling with tension and fear. Behind him the operator was repeating over and over again, his voice desperate, '*Hello, this is Sunray . . . Hello, this is Sunray . . . Do you read me, Big Friend . . . Do you read me . . .?*'

In the very same instant that the barrage ceased with startling suddenness, as if someone had clicked off a giant electric switch, a whistle shrilled. The Vulture started. The French attack had commenced. Almost immediately, the infantry moved out. Crouched low, they began their cautious progress up both sides of the street. At once firing broke out from the first houses. The ugly light of the false dawn was split by the scarlet flashes of rifles. Here and there a Frenchman cried out with pain and crashed down on the pavement, but still the rest came on. The Vulture swallowed hard, trying desperately to control his pounding heart, and took aim once more.

Suddenly he had the flame-thrower operator in his sights. He hesitated no longer. He grabbed at the trigger. The rifle butt slapped back hard into his shoulder. '*Shit!*' he cursed as he saw the tracer slap into the wall half a metre above the operator's head.

Next moment his bodyguards swept in front of the man, while he ignited the tube, falling back to both sides one instant later.

For one long second nothing happened. Then abruptly there was a great hushed intake of air that reminded The Vulture of some huge primeval monster. A greedy purple tongue of oil-tinged flame shot out twenty metres. In a flash it had wrapped itself around the house opposite. There was the crack of bursting windows. Men screamed hysterically. At once the whole house was on fire. Grenadiers, their uniforms ablaze, came running out of the burning exit, screaming in panic-stricken fear.

The operator pressed the trigger of his terrible weapon again. The long tongue of flame engulfed the grenadiers. Even behind the protection of the wall, The Vulture could feel the searing, all-consuming heat. He opened his mouth and, gasping for air, automatically closed his eyes. When he opened them again, all that was left of his grenadiers were a few lumps of charred flesh.

Consumed by a murderous rage at the fate of his men, he pressed the trigger of his rifle. Again the tracer bullet slapped into the wall above the operator's head. Immediately the bodyguards fired a wild burst in the direction of the house in which he was sheltering. The Vulture ducked, feeling wood and stone splinters rip open his face, as the salvo tore holes in the wall. Next instant, the operator, his clumsy pack jumping up and down on his back, was running towards The Vulture's retreat, accompanied by his bodyguards, firing from the hip as they came.

The Vulture, knowing now what his fate was going to be, snapped off two swift shots. The bigger of the two body-guards dropped his machine-pistol, grabbed at his stomach and crashed to the cobbles the next moment. But the other two dived behind a low wall only fifty metres away from the house. In a minute, the operator, once he recovered his wind, would begin to burn them out.

'OPERATOR!' The Vulture screamed for the radio-man, his nerve snapping. 'WHAT?'

'*Nothing . . . nothing . . .*'

The Vulture broke off as the terrible searing tongue of flame licked towards them again. His mouth opened like a stranded fish, gasping in its last death throes. He felt the small hairs at the back of his neck singe. Suddenly there was the stink of burning flesh.

Behind him in the crowded room, the grenadiers were going crazy. Screaming and foaming at the mouth like idiots, eyes wild with absolute, uncontrollable fear, they fought each other to get to the opposite wall, trampling the wounded to death under their boots in their unreasoning panic. The radio operator was toppled from his stool, earphones still attached to his head. The handsome young aide, a gaping shrapnel wound in his chest through which the fine-grey pulsating lung could be seen, had his face smashed in. Another already dead grenadier was seized by a terrified youngster and held up in front of him as a kind of shield. Others simply crouched in a tight, shaking ball like children trying to protect themselves against some horrific nightmare.

The flame-thrower hissed again. Before The Vulture's fascinated gaze, the wall turned a frightening, glowing red. The heat was tremendous. It dragged the very air from his lungs, leaving him suddenly gasping like an ancient asthmatic.

'*Surrender!*' someone screamed. '*We've got to surrender!*'

'*Don't* – ' The Vulture gasped.

Too late. Already half a dozen of his terror-stricken grenadiers were fighting to open the kitchen door, shoving and pushing, scrabbling madly with each other in their haste to run down the stone-flagged corridor and surrender outside. They did not get far. In the same moment that they opened the smouldering front door, its paint seared off in great bubbling blisters, the flame-thrower operator swung his weapon round and fired once more.

Horrifying screams filled the kitchen as their burning bodies shrivelled up in an instant, blackened claws, once petrified hands, reaching upwards, as if trying to climb an invisible ladder to escape the holocaust.

'Sir!' The radio operator's voice cut into the awful silence which followed those screams. 'Sir . . . I've got Big Friend! He's directly above and wants orders.'

The Vulture's heart leaped. It was their last chance. 'BOMB!' he screamed. 'TELL HIM TO BOMB – NOW!'

The operator yelled the message into the radio. Almost instantly, the crackle of flames from the burning houses and the snap-and-crack of small arms fire was drowned by the sirens of the diving Stukas, throwing themselves out of the dawn sky at four hundred kilometres an hour to hit the massed French troops.

The first salvo of fifty-kilo bombs erupted at the far end of the village. The French were caught completely by surprise, not believing that the Boche would dare to bomb their own positions. They stopped their attack, standing there in the battle-littered street, clearly outlined by the flames, wondering what to do next.

It was the opportunity that The Vulture had been waiting for. He loosed off one last desperate shot. It hit the operator. In that same moment, swung right round by the impact of the slug, the Frenchman pressed the trigger of his weapon. A thick cloud of oily flame enveloped the surprised infantry. They went down everywhere, screaming piteously, their uniforms on fire, their helmets glowing dully. The operator sank to his knee, trying to hold on to his weapon. To no avail. As he hit the cobbles, blood pumping from his holed chest, it fell to the ground and lay there, gasping and dribbling flame across the street like a mortally wounded monster.

The Vulture seized the opportunity offered him. Raising his cane, he cried, 'Operator, signal the tanks. Advance all along the front!'

'Sir!'

'And you,' The Vulture commanded his remaining grenadiers, their faces clearly showing that they could hardly believe that they had been saved from a terrible death at the very last moment, 'to the attack. Follow me!'

In a wild rush, abruptly eager for revenge, the young men of *SS Assault Battalion Wotan* stormed straight through the door and smashed head-on into the still dazed French infantry, slashing and stabbing with their bayonets.

SEVEN

'Now!' Schulze hissed, as the Stukas, some two kilometres away, started to drop so startlingly out of the dawn sky, their high-pitched, screaming sirens drowning all other sound.

Matz needed no urging. 'With you!' he called and doubled after Schulze. Together they ran, any noise they made drowned by the rise and fall of the gull-winged dive bombers which were plastering the French village on the horizon. They ran by the cookhouse from which the warm, rich smell of fresh coffee emanated.

'Here,' Schulze cried and flung open the door of a barn. He recoiled the next instant.

He had entered an emergency field hospital. The place was crowded with French wounded. At the far end of the barn, a surgeon was operating by the flickering light of a candle, seemingly up to his knees in sawn-off limbs, his white apron red with blood. He saw the two intruders at once. Above the tight gauze mask, his eyes filled with fear.

'*Freeze!*' Schulze ordered.

If the surgeon did not understand the German word, he understood the gesture. Schulze jerked up his Schmeisser menacingly. The doctor thrust up his hands, bloody scalpel still clasped between nerveless fingers.

His orderly was not so frightened. Instinctively, perhaps, he flung the fine-toothed bone-saw he was holding at Schulze. The Hamburger ducked. Matz cursed angrily as the saw hit him in the face. Almost without knowing it, he pressed the trigger of his machine-pistol. It burst into violent life, filling the crowded room with its staccato chatter. The blast at that close range flung both the orderly and the surgeon against the opposite wall, their chests ripped open. Slowly they slid down the wall, leaving a bloody trail behind them, while the wounded *poilus* screamed with terror.

'Shit!' Schulze cursed. 'Now we've really put our feet in the fat-jar! Make dust, Matz!' He fired a swift burst at the candle. It was swept off the table, plunging the whole place into panic-stricken darkness. Together they ran out as the ether bottles punctured by the burst started to explode.

A fat, unshaven cook with a ladle in his hand barred their way. '*Qu' est-ce-*'

Matz kicked him hard. He went reeling back, screaming with pain, grabbing at his ruined crotch.

'What kind of piggery is this?' a voice cried to Schulze's right.

The big Hamburger swung round, firing from the hip as he did so. The man's face disappeared in a mess of red splinters. They ran on. Slugs started to stitch a wild blue pattern at their heels, coming from a window some twenty metres away. Matz pulled out his sole incendiary grenade and, pausing momentarily, lobbed it into the window. Glass crashed as it exploded. A man fell out, screaming piteously, his body already afire as the phosphorous ignited. He staggered towards the two Germans, his face hideously contorted, his burning arms extended in a plea for help. He did not get far. He tumbled over a munition box and lay there prostrate, his head wreathed in flame. One moment later the munition box exploded with a roar.

Von Dodenburg's heart leapt. Instinctively, he knew that sudden snap and crackle of small arms fire outside indicated that *Wotan* had somehow come to his rescue. He dropped the heel-plate from his bleeding hand and shouted wildly, 'Wotan, I'm here . . . *Wotan, rally on me!*'

The door was flung open. It was the Alsatian, his dark face twisted with both rage and fear.

Von Dodenburg's cry died on his lips as the man raised his long, old-fashioned rifle, with the spiked bayonet attached.

'What are you going to do?' he quavered.

'I don't want to, Captain, but I have orders.'

'What – '

The question died on von Dodenburg's lips as the Sergeant thrust at him. He yelped with pain as the bayonet plunged through his extended right arm and pinned him against the wall.

The Sergeant's prominent Adam's apple rose and fell as he summoned up the last of his courage to carry out the Major's final order – to kill the prisoner if he attempted to escape or if the Germans broke through.

Von Dodenburg knew the look. He had seen it often enough in battle these last few weeks. The man was out to slaughter him. He watched, fascinated as the knuckles whitened over the trigger. In one moment he, von Dodenburg, would be blasted into eternity.

'I must do it,' the Sergeant hissed. 'I must . . . *for France.*' He caught his breath, his eyelids fluttering madly, his jaw tightening as he began that final, fatal squeeze of the trigger.

Von Dodenburg tensed and prepared for the end.

'Please, pray – ' the Sergeant began, as Schulze hurtled through the open door and smashed into the Frenchman with all his strength. The man was thrown to the ground, leaving his bayonet still stuck in von Dodenburg's shoulder. Next instant, Schulze smashed his heavy, hob-nailed boot into the Sergeant's upturned face.

It was then that Captain von Dodenburg fainted.

'*Make my back crack . . . make my knees freeze . . . make my liver quiver . . .*'

Von Dodenburg awoke to Matz's drunken song and a rumbling sound, which he could not make out for a moment. He blinked his eyes a couple of times, feeling the pain in his roughly bandaged shoulder, then saw what was making the strange noise.

Matz was pushing him unsteadily down the cobbled country road in a handcart, drinking out of a bottle of looted French champagne as he did so. Behind him, Schulze marched, his massive shoulders hung with half a dozen rifles. A bottle was clutched in his big ham of a hand, and he boasted – of all things – a pair of flame-red lace knickers on his head instead of a helmet. Together, they herded a bunch of sorry-looking French prisoners, each of them carrying a crate of wine on his shoulders.

In spite of his wounded shoulder, von Dodenburg could not help laughing. Schulze looked, for all the world, like some nineteenth-century explorer setting out for the interior of Darkest Africa together with his native porters.

'Will you not stop that racket?' von Dodenburg commanded the singing Matz with mock testiness. 'And give your commanding officer a drink. His mouth feels like the bottom of a parrot's cage!'

Schulze beamed at him. 'Pop to, you dirty little fart,' he bellowed at Matz. 'Didn't you hear the CO?'

Matz clicked his fingers at the nearest French prisoner. '*Champagne!*' he commanded.

Wearily, as if he had been doing this for a long time now, the French prisoner reached into the crate and handed Schulze a bottle, then bent his head patiently.

Schulze smashed the neck on the back of the man's helmet and tossed the bottle to Matz, who caught it expertly, wiped the bits of glass off with his sleeve and tendered it reverently to von Dodenburg. 'Champagne, as ordered, sir!' he barked.

Von Dodenburg shook his head in mock wonder and took a deep draught of the wine. It tasted good. He took another drink, while the little procession came to a halt behind him. 'Well,' he demanded finally, 'what happened?'

'We won,' Matz answered, smiling down at him like a fond mother looking at her favourite child. 'The Frog line is broken. They've given up.'

'Everywhere?'

'Everywhere,' Matz replied. 'The war's over. We're going to live like God in France* – *but, I mean, for real!*' He waved his bottle happily. 'The war's over. *La Guerre est finis,*' he

---

* A favourite German expression for having a good time.

yelled at the downcast prisoners. '*Soldat allemands* make plenty jig-jig *avec mamselles*.' He thrust his thumb between his two grubby forefingers in an obscene gesture. '*Beaucoup* jig-jig, Frogs. *Compris?*'

'Great God and all his triangles, Matz, will you never hold yer water,' Schulze bellowed, then turned to his CO. 'There's only one thing, sir.'

'What is it?' von Dodenburg asked happily, feeling the champagne now. 'Come on, you big rogue, spit it out. What have you done now?'

'Well, sir, it's a bit hard to explain . . . We might have won the war, but,' he hesitated and then blurted it out, 'we've gone and lost a Mark III.'

'What – *lost* a tank!'

'Right, sir. The Vulture will have my eggs for this.'

'Don't worry, you stupid great turnip,' Matz interrupted, too drunk to care now. 'We'll find The Vulture another one, somewhere or other.'

And with that, the strange, drunken little procession set off again to find what was left of *SS Assault Battalion Wotan*.

Two: The Escape

'I, like you, must escape. And because I must escape, I *will* escape.'

General Gilles, July 1940

ONE

'*Morning soldiers!*' Major Geier, The Vulture, rasped.

'*Morning, Major!*' a thousand young voices roared back, sending the crows nesting in the trees that lined the barrack square rising to the azure Mediterranean sky in hoarse protest.

The Vulture fingered the new laurel leaves on his Knight's Cross, as if to reassure himself that they were still there, before turning to The Butcher. 'Stand the men at ease, Sergeant-Major,' he commanded. 'I want to talk to them this morning.'

'Sir!' The Butcher bellowed, as if The Vulture were standing a thousand metres away from him instead of ten. He wheeled round on his heels and pumped up his chest, his face brick-red, his little pig's eyes scrutinizing the battalion. But he could find no fault. Every man, veteran and new recruit, was standing rigidly at attention, gaze fixed unwaveringly on some distant horizon. 'Battalion!' he roared, so that the word echoed and re-echoed across the barrack square. 'Battalion – *stand at ease*. Stand easy!'

One thousand right feet shot out at the regulation angle. One thousand pairs of eyes resumed their normal expression. One thousand pairs of lungs breathed a sigh of relief. And in the rear rank of the battalion somebody farted. Long, low, lyrically.

The Butcher flushed crimson, his big fists suddenly clenched angrily, as his piglike eyes searched the ranks for the offender. It did not take long to find him. It was that big Hamburger, Schulze, staring at the ground in mock innocence, looking as if butter would not melt in his mouth.

45

The Butcher swore a terrible oath to himself: he would have Schulze's ugly arse before this month was out. Then he turned and reported the parade ready and waiting to The Vulture.

Major Geier touched his peaked cap with his cane in acknowledgement. 'Thank you, Sergeant-Major,' he rasped.

For a long moment he surveyed his men with ice-blue eyes, slowly slapping his crop against his gleaming right boot as if he would have liked to have used it on the waiting troopers. Speaking out of the side of his mouth, Schulze whispered to Matz, 'Look at the little bow-legged bastard, he's working himself up again.'

'Knock it off,' Matz whispered back, his eyes on the little officer. 'If he hears you, he'll ram that cane up yer hairy arse. You know the little sod's temper.'

'At all events, dogs don't shit rubber balls,' Schulze said sagely, obviously, or so the baffled Matz thought, expressing some private philosophy.

'Soldiers,' The Vulture began, 'we have two tasks here in southern France until the High Command, in its wisdom – ' he wrinkled his monstrous beak of a nose in a sneer to indicate just what he thought of the High Command's wisdom – 'decides to move *Wotan* elsewhere. Firstly, we are to seal off this stretch of coast. There are Tommies everywhere in France, trying to save their skins, escaping to Spain or across the water to North Africa. There are some foolish Frogs, too, who haven't yet realized they have lost the war. We must ensure that they remain here – and learn the advantages of German – er – Culture.' He chuckled at his own joke.

The Butcher, always ready to pander to the CO, gave a hearty belly laugh in support and cried: 'That's a good one, sir. *German culture! Ha, ha!*'

Next to Matz, Schulze gave a low raspberry and said, 'That Metzger, he's a right old brown-noser, isn't he? If he didn't have his name on his boot soles, they'd never know who he was – the distance he gets up the CO's arse!'

The Vulture's slight smile vanished, to be replaced by a look of boundless contempt. 'Task number two,' he barked, 'is to train. Train, train, train!' His voice rose in sudden anger, his thin, birdlike face flushing with rage. 'You think you are soldiers. *You are mistaken!* You think you won the war because you were better than the Frogs. *You are mistaken!* You think you are going to have an easy time here in France, with women and wine and all the rest of your nasty piggeries. *You are mistaken!*'

He paused and gasped for breath at the outburst, his eyes running along the front rank of the young soldiers with such an intensity that some of them shivered visibly with apprehension. The Vulture slapped his cane loudly against his right boot. 'One, you are not soldiers. You are a bunch of crazy chimney-sweeps, idle wet-tails, whore's piss in stale beer. *Understand?*' he bellowed.

'We understand, Major!' a thousand voices replied.

'Two.' Again The Vulture slapped his cane against his boot to emphasize the point. 'You didn't beat the Frogs because you were better men. You beat them because they allowed themselves to be beaten. At that village last week, most of you grenadiers were ready to cream your filthy drawers. Some of you probably even did. And one of the tank crews even abandoned a Mark III. By God and Adolf Hitler, if I find those tankers, if I find those men, I'll have the nuts off them.'

'Oh, holy strawsack,' Matz quavered, 'I'm putting in for a posting, toot-sweet.'

'So you are not soldiers and you're certainly not brave. *Understand?*'.

'We understand, Major!' the battalion roared back dutifully.

'So, what are we going to do?' Again the Vulture slapped his cane against his boot in anger. 'Three. We are not going to whore around. We are not going to stick our filthy carrots in grubby Frog females. Further, we are not going to fill our fat guts with suds or Frog wine, wasting our time in cafés and similar establishments. We are going to train, train, *train*. We are going to train so hard that even the most lecherous of you men will consider yourself lucky if you can raise enough strength to play with the five-fingered widow. *Understand?*'

'We understand, Major!'

The Vulture took a deep breath and pointed his riding crop challengingly at the battalion. 'I'm going to either make you or break you. What is it the old soldiers say? War is hell, but peacetime will kill you. Well, in your case, that is going to be true, if you don't learn how to soldier. And by the devil, I'm going to have the finest battalion in the whole of the Armed *SS*, which means in the whole of the Greater German Army, *or else* – '

He left the rest of his threat unspoken, his skinny little body shaking with rage, his ice-blue gaze boring into the scared young recruits' faces.

He swung round suddenly to confront an open-mouthed Sergeant-Major Metzger, who had seen The Vulture pull some scenes in the three years they had served together, but never one like this. 'Sergeant-Major!' he rasped.

'Sir!' The Butcher sprang to attention.

'Take them away. I can't bear the sight of their horrid, unscrubbed faces any longer, Sergeant-Major.' His voice rose hysterically. 'Take them out of my sight and bring them back trained soldiers – *or dead!*'

With that he stalked away in his overlarge riding boots and enormous breeches, shaking his head, as if in profound sorrow, as he did so, and leaving the parade to The Butcher.

The Butcher took his time. He knew von Dodenburg was watching him, but he did not care. In the battalion, it was The Vulture only who made the wet-tails jump through their little hoops, no one else. 'All right, you pack of pregnant penguins,' he snarled, an evil grin on his broad face at the prospect of what was to come, 'you heard what the CO said. From now on it's going to be march or croak in *SS Assault Battalion Wotan*.' For a moment he let his gaze rest on Schulze's insolent face. 'And you'd better learn that – *all of you!* Because if you don't, they'll be sending your miserable bones back to the Fatherland in an orange box.' His massive chest puffed up as if it were going to explode at any moment. 'Parade – *parade, dismiss!*'

Corporal Schulze farted once more, with cool contempt.

TWO

The Toff raised his head from the bracken and peered down carefully at the road block.

'Well?' Tiddey-Oggy demanded in his Portsmouth accent, 'don't keep us in suspense, you public-school prick. Are they Jerries or not?'

The Toff screwed up his eyes against the glare of the sun and surveyed the little barrier, in front of which a line of shabby refugees from the north stood patiently. He could make out the summer kahki of a French gendarme. But were there any Germans checking the civvies' documents, too?

Suddenly the sun glinted and almost blinded him. He turned his head quickly.

'What's up?' Tonsils came forward. He was the third member of the 'Terrible Triplets', as they had once been known in the 2nd Battalion the Scots Guards before it had surrendered to the Germans at St Valery, two weeks before. 'Jerries?'

The Toff rolled over on his back and nodded glumly. 'Jerries. Military police to be exact. I caught a glimpse of those silver dog-collars their redcaps wear.'

'Ballocks, that's torn it,' Tiddey-Oggy said.

Gloomily the three comrades lay on their backs in the hot bracken and wondered what to do next. On the run for the last fourteen days, since they had refused their CO's order to lay down arms, they had been steadily working their way through France, in an effort to reach neutral Spain and freedom.

The three youths – The Toff, so named on account of his public-school accent; Tiddey-Oggy, whose favourite dish was Cornish pasty, or 'tiddey-oggy' in his native Portsmouth; and Tonsils, who spoke in a swift, rasping Cockney voice – had discovered the tricks of escaping swiftly. Out on a night march a rye field gave the best cover because the furrows were wider apart than in wheatfields. Damp woods, especially if they were made up of oaks, were not for sleeping in, unless you were one of the many mosquitoes they harboured. Seed potatoes made good eating, even raw. They had learned things they had never expected to need to know when they had volunteered for the Guards a year before.

Now the ragged youths knew their luck was beginning to run out. For the first time since they had begun their escape, they had been refused food by the French. That morning a Frenchman to whom they had appealed for food had told them '*Les Allemands sont des gens tout-a-fait aimables*' and had advised them to give themselves up. 'Ballocks,' Tiddey-Oggy had exclaimed, giving his standard reply to most things, when The Toff had finished translating the swarthy Frenchman's words. The Toff had persisted in his begging, however, until the civilian had gone into his dirty little house and returned, not with food as they had anticipated, but with a cocked fowling rifle in his hand. '*La guerre est finie*,' he had snarled, ordering them off his property. They had slunk away, with their empty stomachs 'doing back-flips with hunger,' according to Tonsils.

Hunger was not their only problem. All that morning they had been encountering enemy road-blocks. Twice they had nearly stumbled into a German trap, escaping at only the very last moment, and once they had spotted a young British lieutenant, his left trouser leg completely torn away and his pale face a mass of stubble and scratches, swaying back and forth, in the last stages of exhaustion, as his grinning German captors searched him.

Tonsils, the quick-witted Cockney, put all their thoughts into words as they lay there, weary, miserable and desperately hungry. 'I think the Jerries have got us by the goolies, lads.'

'You're not thinking of surrendering?' The Toff asked in alarm.

'Ballocks to that,' Tiddey-Oggy growled.

50

'Ner, that ain't it for me, mate. But we can't keep on running like this, Toff, with no grub in our guts. You saw how we nearly ran right slap-bang into the Jerries that last time. It ain't on, mate. We've got to try something else.'

'What would you suggest then, Tonsils?' The Toff asked in his most upper-class manner, raising himself on one elbow to look at the sun-burnt, emaciated face of the red-headed Cockney.

'Move back a few miles, because it looks to me that they've got a line of roadblocks to stop anybody moving south to the sea, to that place Nîmes we were heading for.'

'Bugger that for a tale!' the third guardsman growled. 'It's taken me all me strength to get this far. Go back, ballocks!'

'Now listen,' Tonsils said urgently, 'today we got to get some grub. Whether we beg for it or half-inch it, I don't care, but we've gotta. And we're not gonna get it thata way. So we go back.'

'I see what you mean, Tonsils,' The Toff agreed, smoothing back his long, sleek hair. 'But what then?'

'Search me, mate,' Tonsils shrugged eloquently. 'Perhaps when we break through the squareheads' line, we can nick a boat at Nîmes and sail along the coast to Spain instead of doing it on our plates-o'-meat.' He looked across at Tiddey-Oggy's grumpy red face. 'You're allus rabbiting on about yer old man being a chief petty officer in the Royal, so you should be able to sail a boat.'

The other man pursed his lips thoughtfully. 'Well, as it so happens, I have sailed a bit in the Solent. I mean, nothing fancy like you public school twits sail,' – he looked at The Toff – 'but I know how to handle a sailboat – '

'All right, mate, don't give us yer sodding life-story,' Tonsils interrupted. 'Sell it to the *News of the World* when we get back to Blighty. First things first. *Grub!*'

'*Grub* is the operative word,' The Toff agreed firmly. He exhaled hard and, using his hands, pressed his weary body up from the hot bracken. 'Well, chaps, what do you say, shall we be on our way?'

'Ballocks to that leader-of-men public-school shit,' Tiddey-

51

Oggy grumbled. All the same, he made the effort.

With a weary, heartfelt groan, Tonsils did the same. Five minutes later, the three men in their tattered, dirt-stained khaki were marching back the way they had come.

Totally exhausted, light-headed with fatigue and hunger, and unable to concentrate or to focus their eyes on the objects around them, the three comrades staggered through the moonlit wood like drunken men.

The Toff in the lead was in a complete daze, haunted by feverish dreams of a soft bed – complete with spotless white linen – and his grandmother's groaning dinner table back at her seat in Gloucestershire. He staggered through the oaks, guided solely by the sparkling, dew-wet meadow to his right beyond the wood, and led the Terrible Triplets out of the cover of the wood and into an open field before he even realized it. He stopped in alarm, while at the rear Tonsils hissed angrily, 'You silly git, now look what you've gone and done.'

The Toff froze in alarm. To their right there was a little house, which he had completely overlooked, its door was open, and someone was standing in the doorway, staring straight at them. 'What do we do?' he asked. 'Run for it?'

'Ballocks,' Tiddey-Oggy cursed. 'I couldn't run now if Hitler himself was after me.'

'Yer, yer right. Toff, try him for some grub. I can't go another step as it is.'

'OK, but be it on your head,' The Toff said. Wearily he began to make his way across the damp field towards the watching civilian, who neither moved nor spoke.

'Good evening,' The Toff said in French, staring at the short, thick-set man of about fifty smoking a pipe, whose dark eyes revealed nothing.

'Good evening,' he answered, without removing the pipe from his mouth, and waited.

A little helplessly, The Toff began the routine he had grown accustomed to these last weeks, though he came from a family which would have been appalled had they known that their son was begging.

The Frenchman listened attentively and wordlessly to his account of how they made their escape from St Valery and how they intended to reach Spain. 'We need food . . .'

The Frenchman nodded in understanding and, with a jerk of his head, indicated that they should enter the house.

Five minutes later they were wolfing down a meal of cheese and bread, well washed down with *vin ordinaire*, while their host puffed gently at his pipe and watched them carefully, as if he were looking for something special in their faces. Finally he seemed to make up his mind about whatever was worrying him; he indicated the door to the next room with a jab of his pipe, saying 'Sleep,' and disappeared through the front door without another word.

'Funny old bugger,' Tiddey-Oggy said through a mouthful of bread and cheese. 'Don't know what to make of him.' Belching, he reached for his mug of wine.

The Toff wiped the crumbs from the crisp white bread off his mouth delicately and nodded his agreement. 'Yes, he is a bit of a strange type.'

Tonsils drained the last of his wine. 'He can be as nutty as a fruitcake as far as I'm concerned, but I'm gonna get some kip. Can't hardly keep me peepers open. Ta, ta,' he said, staggering over to the other room.

'But what if he's gone to give us up to the Germans?' The Toff protested to Tiddey-Oggy.

'Silly bugger, Toff. That shows you public-school types don't know yer arse from yer elbow. He wouldn't have fed us first, would he? For the working class, grub don't grow on trees. Yer've got to have money to pay for it. If yer so worried, you can stand first stag while I have a bit of shut-eye. Wake me in an hour and I'll take over. Christ, am I beat!' He wandered off to the other room from which Tonsils' heavy snores were already coming, leaving a puzzled Toff alone at the abandoned table.

The Toff woke with a start. The man with the pipe was shaking him by the shoulder.

'What, what the devil – ' he began thickly, but he stopped when he became aware of a man standing next to the civilian.

The stranger was very tall, with a great beak of a nose dominating a commanding face which was accustomed, The Toff realized at once, to giving orders – and having them obeyed. He waited until the sleep-drunken Toff had properly opened his eyes, then he said, 'My name is Gilles. I am a general in the French Army.' He paused and then spoke in English. 'I, like you, must escape – and because I must escape – ' his dark eyes glowed feverishly ' – I *will* escape.' He said the words as if they were an article of faith. 'And you will help me. All we have to do is break through the *SS* battalion now stationed at Nîmes.'

From the bedroom, Tiddey-Oggy breathed, 'Ballocks! Is *that* all?'

THREE

'*Crap-asses! Horrible slack arses! Sloppy shit-shovellers! Garden dwarfs! Arses with ears! Brainless barn-shitters! Whores' piss!*' The Butcher's voice rose to a crescendo. '*Soldiers like you – I've shit 'em for breakfast! You lot I can use like a fist in the eye!*'

Lying face down in the burning sand, his gigantic frame shaking with the effort, Schulze gasped, 'And that's what the shit'll get from me one dark night, mark my words, Matz.'

'Save . . . save . . . your breath,' his running mate managed to whisper, wheezing like an ancient asthmatic.

For the past thirty minutes, The Butcher had been playing what he called 'beach-games' with them. After ordering each man to be laden down with a thirty-kilo pack of stones, he had them hopping around in the deep sand, with their rifles extended straight out in front of them, until they became dizzy with exhaustion. Then there had been the 'attack under fire': run five paces, down, up, run another five paces, down and up time and time again so that their uniforms were black with sweat and their breath came in frantic, wrenching gasps.

Now it was 'pumping'. 'Think you've got a nice pneumatic blonde underneath yer – those of you aspagarus Tarzans who like girls,' The Butcher had bellowed happily. 'And then you begin pumping up and down as if you're giving her a real, red-hot piece of sausage. *Pumping begin!*'

That first session of press-ups seemed to last for an eternity. The Butcher had no mercy on them. '*Up – down, up – down!*' Their straining arms fought to move the weight on their backs, as the sweat poured from them, eyes bulged out of crimson faces and breath rasped from their tortured chests. '*Up – down . . . up-down . . .*'

When at last the order to stop was given, they collapsed, burying their sweat-lathered faces in the burning sand, not hearing The Butcher's obscene tirade and aware of nothing save the burning pain that swept through their arms and legs, whose muscles trembled uncontrollably.

Now the murderous torture was to begin once again.

'All right, you grimy bunch of greenbeaks, let's be having you!' The Butcher's voice penetrated their pain-racked daze. 'Ready for another little beach-game.' As his voice rose in a sudden fury, the veins bulged purple at his temples and his broad face flushed an ugly red. 'Pumping – *pumping commence!*'

The troopers started to raise and lower their bodies once more. Happily The Butcher swaggered through the ranks, pressing a heavy boot on a back here and there and bearing down with all his weight when he thought some miserable, sweat-blinded soldier was not pressing down low enough, then laughing uproariously when the soldier collapsed in the sand.

Schulze knew he was in for trouble when he spotted The Butcher's big, highly polished jackboots poised in front of his face. He pretended not to notice them, pumping easily now, his strength returned as anger – at The Butcher, the battalion, the war, this torture – lent him new energy.

'Doing pretty well for a warm brother, aren't you, Schulze?' The Butcher said quietly, a deceptive, menacing softness in his voice now.

The big Hamburger continued the exercise, feeling his muscles working as if they were oiled steel springs, his breathing well under control now.

'Perhaps you ain't got enough weight in yer pack? Been up to your usual nasty tricks, Schulze,' The Butcher said in that same soft threatening tone.

Schulze tensed. He knew what was going to happen. His big jaw hardened. The Butcher wasn't going to get him down. He stiffled a groan of pain as the Sergeant-Major's heavy boot bore down on the small of his back.

'You ain't risking much of a big lip now, Schulze,' The Butcher grunted, pressing hard. 'Where's the witty little remark, eh? Come on, comedian speak up.' He pressed harder.

Schulze bit his bottom lip till his mouth filled with the salty taste of blood, but he continued pumping.

The Butcher bore down with his full weight. Schulze tensed his massive shoulder muscles and pumped on, sweat streaming from his tortured muscles, his arms feeling as if they were to be ripped from their sockets at any moment and his leg muscles afire with agony.

Abruptly the terrible weight was removed. Schulze gasped a broken sob of relief. Only half-consciously did he hear the metallic noise of the NCO's well-oiled dirk being removed from its scabbard.

The Butcher was lying down on the burning sand facing him, his piglike features contorted with rage. He thrust his dirk directly underneath Schulze's heaving chest. 'Now,' he commanded through gritted teeth, 'let's have three last ones – at the double! I hope you shittingly well break down because nothing would give me more pleasure in this world, Schulze, than to plunge this blade into your insolent black heart. Pumping begin. *One!*'

Schulze bore down, the gleaming dirk only a matter of millimetres from his heart, while all around the relieved troopers watched the terrible little scene in awesome anticipation. Desperately he fought to rise again, knowing that if he failed to make a straight, clean upwards thrust, his muscles would collapse and he would fall directly on to the dirk. Sweat pearls streaming down his forehead and blinding him, his breath coming in great rasping sobs, he managed to rise.

The Butcher licked his thick ugly lips, his face flushed with rage and disappointment. 'Well,' he tormented Schulze, 'you did it once. Do you think you'll be lucky a second time? *Two!*'

Schulze prayed for the first time ever since he had been kicked out of St Adelheid's Junior School for trying to look up a nun's skirt. Slowly, ever so slowly, he came down, his arms wobbling frighteningly, his wild-bulging eyes full of the dirk, his hands threatening to give way underneath him at any moment, his breath caught deep in his fiercely parched throat. Now a mere hair's-breadth separated him from the sharp point of the dirk. He dug his teeth deep into his bottom lip, cutting right through it. With the last of his strength, he began to raise himself once more.

'Come on, Schulze,' The Butcher hissed, 'let go. You know you can't make it . . . Come on, it's all over for you anyway . . . *Let go . . . Let go!*'

Red and silver stars started to explode in front of Schulze's eyes. Of their own volition, his powerful arms began to tremble violently. He knew he was going to black out. He wasn't going to make it. Desperately he tried to fight off the blackness which threatened to overcome him.

'Come on, Schulze,' The Butcher sneered, 'I thought you were a packet of muscles who could never be worn down. Come on, big-mouth, get it up, or there's going to be a nasty training accident. Come on!'

Schulze knew he was at the end of his strength. He fought to raise himself but couldn't. He was going to fall on to the evil blade.

'Sergeant-Major, that's enough!' A familiar voice cut into the hecticly-gasping silence. 'Stop it at once. *At once! Do you hear?*'

In the same instant that Schulze collapsed into the sand, missing the hastily removed dirk by millimetres, he recognized the voice which had saved him. It was that of Captain von Dodenburg.

'But, sir,' Captain von Dodenburg protested hotly as he and The Vulture resumed their walk along the dead-straight beach road which led to Nîmes, leaving the grateful troopers and a crest-fallen Metzger behind them, 'one trains men to live, not to be killed. That fool Metzger could have killed Corporal Schulze with that damned trick just now.'

The Vulture faced him, his monstrous beak of a nose red and peeling from the Mediterranean sun. 'You are a sentimentalist, von Dodenburg,' he rasped. 'Men are always killed in training. It has always been that way – in the Imperial Army, the *Reichswehr** and in the present Greater German Army. One can't make an omelette without breaking eggs.'

Captain von Dodenburg, his face still an angry red from the incident they had just witnessed, snapped, 'I disagree, sir. *Strongly*. It has always been the policy of the Armed SS to get away from the old brutal training methods. Reichsführer Himmler has always maintained – '

The Vulture waved his cane for him to stop. 'Spare me the military theories of Reichsführer Himmler, von Dodenburg. When battles are fought from an office in Berlin, I shall listen. At present battles are fought on battlefields.' He whacked his cane against his gleaming boot. 'And I am the one who has to lead that raw rabble into battle. You didn't see how those grenadiers froze in that village when the French trapped us. *I did!* They lost their heads. It will never happen again, not as long as I command *SS Assault Battalion Wotan*.' His voice rose angrily. 'I demand instant, total obedience and that can only be achieved by making the men more afraid of me and of their commanders than they are of the enemy. What do a few casualties matter if that aim is achieved?'

Von Dodenburg knew there was no further arguing with The Vulture.

For a few moments they walked side by side in silence, viewing the deep-blue water to their right, with the heat haze rippling across it as the red ball of the sun reached its zenith. Then The Vulture said, 'Another matter, von Dodenburg. As you know our patrols keep catching Tommies and Frogs trying to leave the south virtually every day now. Fortunately the populace is sick of the war and only too glad to inform on their former allies and on their own countrymen foolish enough to believe that England will continue this war. As if that fat drunkard Churchill could care about the fate of Europe!'

---

* The pre-1933 German Army.

Von Dodenburg nodded. 'I don't know much about Churchill. He looks a fighter to me, sir.'

The Vulture dismissed the new British Prime Minister with a contemptuous wave of his cane. 'Little fish,' he rasped. 'However, High Command has no intention of allowing the French to find some sort of rallying point in their empire or England. There is still a powerful French Colonial Army in North Africa and elsewhere. We cannot afford to allow them to commence some independent military or political course. You understand, von Dodenburg?'

The handsome young Captain nodded, taking his gaze off the little French civilian smoking his pipe in dour silence, who watched the two *SS* officers walk by. He wondered what must be going on in the Frenchman's mind as his dark eyes took in the progression of the bemedalled invaders along his native beach.

'I'm sure you are wondering what this is leading up to, von Dodenburg,' The Vulture continued.

'Yes sir, somewhat,' von Dodenburg agreed.

'The High Command has already learned from its spies in London that one senior French general named de Gaulle – never heard of him myself, but apparently he had some success against us earlier on in the campaign – has made it to the Tommy capital and is going to be used by Churchill as some sort of rallying point for any Frenchman not prepared to accept the fact that France has lost the war. The High Command doesn't think much of the chap. He's a bit of a dreamer, not a man of action. There is, however, another French general still at large somewhere here in southern France who would present much more of a danger to the German cause if he managed to join the Tommies.'

'I see, sir.'

'No, you don't, von Dodenburg,' The Vulture said cynically, 'but you will in a moment.' He ignored the Captain's sudden blush. 'The man's name is Gilles. General Gilles is apparently a hero of Verdun, where he was wounded three times. He was captured there, too, but after two attempts at escape, he finally made it all the way from

Upper Silesia on foot. After the First War, he fought everywhere in the French Empire – Algeria, Morocco, Indo-China. In nineteen thirty-nine he took the French Expeditionary Corps to Norway, and last May he dealt this chap Rommel everyone's talking about these days – ' The Vulture's face wrinkled up in an exclamation of disdain at the upstart Swabian peasant general who had come up so suddenly from nowhere – 'a rather bloody nose, which he won't forget for a long time, on the River Meuse. During the drive south, he was the only French general who really put up any real resistance to us. High Command suspects he was the brain behind our only nasty little affair at the last stopline before Nîmes.'

Von Dodenburg whistled softly. 'Quite a record, sir!'

'Quite a record,' The Vulture echoed, 'and it is one that would pull in recruits, if he got away to London. The General is especially liked by the French Colonial Army in North Africa. Therefore – ' he pulled down the side of his right eye in the German manner to reveal the pink below – 'wooden eye, be on your guard! If General Gilles is in the Nîmes area, as the High Command suspects, he *must* not on any account be allowed to escape. The reputation of the battalion depends upon it. I shall make you personally responsible to stop any attempt of that nature. You understand, von Dodenburg, it will be your head that'll fall, not mine!'

'I understand,' von Dodenburg said grimly, telling himself that, as usual, The Vulture was prepared to ride over the dead bodies of his officers in order to preserve his own reputation and gain those general's stars which were his overriding aim. 'I'll ensure patrols are run along the coast in our sector twenty-four hours a day. I need some details of this – '

'You'll get them, von Dodenburg.' The Vulture cut him short, as if the matter were closed for him now for good. 'Back to more important things. Now this training exercise with live ammunition tomorrow morning . . .'

Thus they passed on their way, leaving the silent man with the pipe staring after their elegantly uniformed backs and telling himself he had just seen the men who would be the ones to attempt to stop General Gilles. Then he laughed, a rare gesture, remembering suddenly how he and the Old Man (as he had always called the General behind his back) had trudged right across Germany in 1918 and still managed to fool the Boche, although neither one of them had spoken a single word of German. No, he told himself as he turned and started trudging off to make his report, the Boche would have to get up early in the day if they wanted to nab General Guy Gilles . . .

FOUR

Corporal Schulze sat in the shade outside the boiling hot cookhouse, his broad peasant face still drawn and haggard from the morning's 'beach-games'. He was busily forming what looked like a long, brown sausage, tossing it back and forth as he moulded it, as if it were very sticky.

Matz, his feet still burning from the long day's training, sat on a three-legged stool, enjoying the cooling sensation of the ice-water into which he kept dipping his feet. With a looted cigar like a small pole stuck between his lips, he stared at his running-mate, puzzled. Finally his curiosity got the best of him. 'What's that, Schulze?'

'What's it look like?' the Corporal answered, not looking up, apparently too engrossed in his task.

'To me – a turd.'

'Exactly.' Schulze surprised him by agreeing with his poor venture at humour.

Matz swiftly took out his cigar, 'What did you say?'

'You heard.'

Matz's mouth fell open. 'What you're doing, playing with shit? You gotta little bird in yer head that goes tweet-tweet? You *meschugge* or something?'

'No,' Schulze answered, still engrossed in his work, while Matz watched him open-mouthed, telling himself the strain and the sun must finally have got to the poor Hamburg bastard. After one year of war, Schulze had gone ape at last.

Schulze completed his task and, placing the brown object on the palm of his big right hand, gazed at it admiringly. Then he ran his nose along it, his nostrils twitching pleasurably as if it exuded a delicate, rare odour. 'Exactly right,' he breathed.

'Shit!' Matz exclaimed in disgust, dropping his cigar in the dust in his excitement. 'I'm gonna get the bone-menders! They'll take you away in a rubber-wagon, Schulze. That sun on the beach and this morning's "fun" was too much for you – you've got air in your tooth, no more cups in yer cupboard. You've turned through. *You're crackers!*'

'You think so, you little wet-dream?' Schulze said softly, looking at his crimson-faced friend calmly but with an unholy light in his honest blue eyes. 'So that's what you think eh?' He lifted the turd-like object and levelled it at Matz, so that the little man cowered away, afraid that the lunatic might smear it on his face. 'But you're wrong, very wrong.' His big jaw hardened. 'You saw what that big bastard of a Butcher tried to do to me this morning, didn't you?'

Matz nodded, unable to speak as the turd was wagged up and down only millimetres away from his nose now.

'If it hadn't have been for the CO, I'd be hearing the sodding angels singing now, I would. Well, Matzi, I'm not going to let that one-time sausage-shitter get away with it! I'm going to shaft him – and shaft him again – until his stupid ass is a bright purple and he'll come to me on his bended knee crying for mercy. By God I am!'

Finding his voice at last, Matz asked, 'What's that got to do with . . . with that?'

Schulze grinned suddenly and placed the turd-like object carefully on the bench on which he sat. 'You know how The Vulture is a stickler for cleanliness, especially in his own quarters. Hell, the lads nearly piss in their pants when they're detailed to do fatigues in his place.'

Matz nodded but said nothing.

'And you know how he's particularly fussy about his thunderbox?'

Matz, wondering what all this was leading up to, nodded again.

'And you know, too, who's in charge of seeing that that thunderbox is picobello-clean before The Vulture carries out his morning inspection?'

'The Butcher?' Matz breathed.

'Exactly! Every morning at ten hundred hours on the dot, after he has his morning ride and breakfast at the officers' casino, The Vulture returns to his quarters to check everything out before he takes off for the day's training. The Butcher waits for him, knowing that once he has finished with The Vulture's quarters, the rest of the day is his.' The big man's burning anger at the NCO thickened his voice. 'Tomorrow morning The Butcher is going to experience a blue wonder, Matz. Mark my words – *a blue wonder!*'

With that he wrapped the turd-like object in a piece of greaseproof paper, stolen from the cookhouse, rose to his feet and strolled away whistling, leaving a mystified Matz staring at his broad back and wondering if he should call in the battalion MO to have a look at his friend after all.

'Come on, you idiots!' The Butcher barked. 'Get your arses out of here. The CO'll be here in five minutes!'

Hurriedly the anxious young latrine-orderlies, burdened down with their buckets, rags and cleaning tackle, disappeared through the door of The Vulture's quarters, leaving Sergeant-Major Metzger alone to carry out his own inspection before The Vulture arrived.

His well-trained eyes swept the living-room, which was spartanly furnished as befitted a Prussian officer's quarters, save for the feminine silken cushions and a portrait of a naked Greek boy next to that of Frederick the Great on the wall. Everything in order, not an item out of place. He ran his white-gloved fingers across the table and inspected the glove. Not a speck of dust anywhere. Satisfied, the big NCO stalked through the door into The Vulture's thunderbox, as the CO preferred to call his bathroom.

Carefully he inspected the wash-basin, looking underneath the taps and checking the metal chain which held the plug. Everything glittered. He nodded his head, satisfied. The wet-tail who had cleaned the wash-basin this morning had worked a good thirty minutes on it. He took a look at himself in the spotless mirror and beamed happily. He looked every inch a senior NCO of the Regular German Army from his monkey-swing,* which indicated that he was an expert shot, to the gleaming tin on his broad chest, down to his mirrorlike dice-beakers. Then he turned his attention to the toilet – the thunderbox itself.

First he examined the wooden lid. It gleamed, its surface scrubbed a brilliant white. He turned his attention to the interior itself, running his practised gaze over the sparkling white china. Not a stain or spot anywhere. He bent down and ran his gloved hand around the upper rim of the bowl. It came away clean. Once The Vulture had carried out the same inspection and his gloved hand had come away with a minute piece of crusted cleaning powder attached to it. The Butcher had thought he was going to have a heart-attack. The Vulture, his face crimson, had cursed for a solid five minutes before ordering the whole orderly crew on extra fatigues for the next month, and then he had tongue-lashed a scared Metzger for a further ten minutes. No, he breathed to himself, recalling the terrible incident now, he was not going to have that happen again. In spite of the hold he had over The Vulture regarding the man's sexual preferences, he knew he must not push the CO too far. The Vulture would get rid of him if he did. Finally he checked the toilet-paper. A full roll. He nodded his satisfaction. Everything was under control. He marched out to wait for the CO at the door to his quarters, not noticing the window beginning to open behind him . . .

'Morning, Sarnt-Major!' The Vulture rasped, striding down the corridor, slapping his riding crop impatiently against the side of his boot.

'Morning, sir!' The Butcher bellowed. The corridor echoed and re-echoed with the noise as he 'built his ape': setting his body rigidly at attention, with his fingers gripped tightly down the seams of his trousers. 'Quarters ready and

* A shoulder lanyard.

prepared for inspection, *sir!*'

The Vulture tapped the side of his rakishly angled cap with his cane. 'Lead on, Sarnt-Major.'

The Butcher stood to one side while The Vulture's sharp gaze swept the living-room, waiting anxiously for the CO's comment.

The Vulture prodded one of the silken cushions with his cane and grunted, 'Excellent . . . Now the thunderbox.'

'This way, sir.' The Butcher extended his right hand, like a hotel manager ushering a rich man into his expensive suite.

The Vulture followed behind in his overlarge boots, the silver spurs which he wore – although he had long left the cavalry for the quicker promotion of the *SS* – jingling.

At the door, The Butcher clicked to attention once more and let the CO get on with his inspection, confident that everything was well under control.

The Vulture carried out the same routine as the NCO had done only moments before, examining every item with meticulous care. As he always told his officers in the casino, 'Gentlemen, my soul might belong to *Wotan*, but my outside plumbing belongs to me. My personal thunderbox is something holy!' The comment usually raised a laugh from the junior officers, but there was no humour in the CO's remark: his thunderbox *was* holy.

Finally The Vulture turned his attention to that holy object on which he spent many an hour of patient waiting. He examined the toilet roll and grunted his approval. The lid was also to his satisfaction. He opened up the lid and recoiled, not able to believe – or so it seemed – what he saw there.

'*Sarnt-Major!*' he gasped, finally managing to speak.

'Sir,' The Butcher began. He caught his breath when he saw the look on the CO's face. Something had gone wrong, terribly wrong. 'What . . . what is it, sir?'

Silently The Vulture beckoned him across with his cane, his other hand still holding up the lid.

Like a condemned man going to the gallows, Metzger crossed the room.

'What do you think that is, Metzger?' The Vulture rasped.

The blood drained from The Butcher's normally brick-red face. 'Why, sir,' he stuttered, 'it . . . it . . . looks like . . .' he gulped. 'Like shit!'

'It *is* shit!'

'But . . .' The Butcher could not find the words to express his horrified surprise.

'Exactly,' The Vulture said icily. 'But how does anyone come to have the audacity to shit in my private thunderbox, eh?'

'I don't know . . . I don't know, sir.'

The Vulture managed to contain himself. He would have liked to slash his cane across the stupid oaf's face, but he remembered in time that the NCO knew too much about his personal life. Instead he said, his voice low and full of menace. 'Don't just stand there, Metzger, get rid of it.'

'But how, sir?' Metzger asked miserably. 'The orderlies took their pans and shovels with them and there isn't – '

'Your hands are big enough.' The Vulture cut him short.
'*My hands!*'

'Your foolish great flippers. Come on, Metzger, get that turd out of there before I make you eat the damned thing. *At the double!*'

Very gingerly, Metzger reached a paw in to touch the horrid object. The Vulture lost patience with him. His boot thudded into the NCO's ribs at the same instant that he touched the turd. Instinctively his fingers closed with the sudden shock and pain. The turd squashed horribly in his hand.

Suspended in mid-action Sergeant-Major Metzger stood bent there, gripping the thing, his face contorted with disgust, not knowing what to do next.

The Vulture made his mind up for him. His riding cane twacked across the NCO's broad shoulders. 'Well, don't just stand there. Get that devilish thing out of my sight – at once! And thank your lucky stars, Metzger, that I can understand you have suffered enough. But, in three devils' name, never let it happen again, or by God – ' He never finished his terrible threat, for suddenly Metzger was in a great hurry to rid himself of the brown goo sticking to his fingers.

All considerations of rank and military courtesy forgotten, Metzger blundered outside. He spotted a patch of grass and ran to it. Frantically, repressing his nausea, he wiped the cunningly prepared mixture of butter and brown sugar off his hands while the two watchers, hidden in the trees beyond, rocked with silent laughter. Then he fled to his own quarters to wash his hands.

Schulze rose and looked down at Matz, his face red with laughter and tears streaming down his wrinkled cheeks. His features suddenly grew grim and purposeful. 'This time we put him in the shit, right and proper. But I've got other things in mind for The Butcher. Come on, short-ass. We're gonna visit the ladies of the town . . .'

FIVE

'Any sign of his nibs, tosher?' Tonsils asked.

The Toff, who had the first stag that night, shook his head and carefully replaced the black-out curtain. It was well past the German curfew time and he did not want to attract any patrols to the lonely woodland cottage.

'Sod it!' Tonsils cursed. 'I'm starved and my tonsils are floating. What I wouldn't give for a sup of wine!'

'There's water.' The Toff attempted to console him.

'Fishes ferk in water, didn't you know that, you public-school prick? But it ain't that, Toff. It's the tension. His nibs promised faithfully he'd be back tonight. He's been gone for forty-eight sodding hours now.' Suddenly the Cockney confidence was gone from his voice. 'What do you think, mate? He ain't gone for a burton, has he?'

For a long moment The Toff did not reply. There was a sudden heavy silence in the tight little cottage, broken only by the rustle of the night breeze outside and the steady snoring of Tiddey-Oggy in the bedroom, interrupted every now and again by sounds like 'Pompey' and 'plenty o' onions'.

Presumably, The Toff told himself, the Portsmouth man was thinking of his native city and the celebrated Cornish pasty that was produced there.

'Well,' Tonsils urged, 'do you think he's gorn and done a bunk on us, leaving us holding the sodding baby?'

Still The Toff did not speak. His high brow creased in a frown, he recalled their last moments with General Gilles and his taciturn, pipe-smoking ex-batman, who had hidden him after the recent French surrender. The General had not looked then as if he were about to run away and leave them in the lurch. He had projected an aura of authority and confidence, which had made the Terrible Triplets square their weary shoulders and bark out 'sir' when they spoke to him, as if they were back at the Guards' Training Depot. He had parted from them with a firm handclasp and a flash of his confident, penetrating eyes, followed by the words, 'Never fear, gentlemen, I will return – with good news for us all!'

'No, Tonsils,' The Toff said at last, 'I trust the General. After all, he is a gentleman – ' The ex-public schoolboy caught himself too late.

'*Gentleman!*' Tonsils sneered, his sharp narrow face contorted in contempt. 'Oh dearie, dearie me. A gentleman. What about Mosley, Toff? He was an upper-class gent, too – and a ruddy great roaring, Jew-baiting, fascist traitor to boot!'

The Toff held his finger to his lips urgently. 'I'm sorry, Tonsils, it just slipped out.'

'Yeah, as the actress said to the bishop,' Tonsils said easily, his face relaxing into a good-humoured grin once more. 'Forget it, Toff. Just letting off steam. I'm a bit het-up, I suppose.'

'We all are. It's the tension. But that French General – he's got an aura about him. I know you'll laugh and say it's old public-school bullshit, but that chap has something about him. I don't know how to explain it exactly, but I'd trust him with my life, like – ' He stopped short abruptly, his bronzed face very tense. 'What's that?' he hissed.

'What's what?' Tonsils' face reflected the other man's sudden alarm.

'Douse the candle – *quick*! Wake up, Tiddey-Oggy! At the double!'

Tonsils heard the vague sounds from outside, too. He blew out the candle. Placing his hand over Tiddey-Oggy's mouth to prevent him from crying out, he whispered urgently, 'T-O, show a leg. There's somebody outside.'

The man's snores ceased immediately and he was awake at once. 'Jerries?' he hissed, grabbing for the section of lead piping he kept beneath the straw-filled pillow.

'Don't know. Toff is checking it out at the window.'

The Toff cautiously parted the curtain once more and peered out into the moonlit meadow that stretched from the lonely cottage to the woods which surrounded it. Someone was definitely moving through the trees. He knew it was not the light breeze which caused the disturbance. Suddenly a dark figure emerged from the trees. The Toff caught his breath, recognizing the coal-scuttle helmet at once. 'Action stations,' he commanded. 'Jerry patrol!'

Silently his lips counted their number as they slipped stealthily from the oaks. '*One . . . two . . . three . . . four . . .*' No more. They were outnumbered by one man. He waited no longer. Taking up his own position behind the door, he held the loop of chicken wire he had prepared for just this emergency in fingers that were suddenly trembling violently.

The three men waited: Tiddey-Oggy snoring once more on the rough bed, with the blanket thrown over his head but the length of lead-piping clutched firmly in his hand; Tonsils ready at the window, prepared to spring out and come up from behind, once the first German entered the cottage; The Toff behind the door with, he could not help thinking at this moment, his very pathetic weapon.

The harsh stamp of heavy jackboots started to come down the gravel path leading to the door. The Toff swallowed hard. On the bed, Tiddey-Oggy began to snore louder. Tonsils held his long knife more firmly in a hand that was suddenly sweating heavily. The boots stopped. A heavy fist pounded on the ancient wooden door. Tiddey-Oggy snored ever louder.

The fact that their knock had not been answered, even though snores shook the remote little cottage, seemed to puzzle the Germans. Behind the door, hardly daring to breathe, The Toff could almost sense their bewilderment. *Would they go away after all?*

The Toff looked down. The door handle began to move. The Jerries were coming in! He tensed as it creaked open. A finger of icy-white light poked into the dark room, darting here and there before it came to rest on Tiddey-Oggy snoring away happily in the makeshift bed.

The German with the torch said something softly to his

companions and they laughed a little, drowning the noise Tonsils made as he rushed through the window. Then, slinging his machine-pistol over his right shoulder as if he had decided the situation was harmless, the German holding the torch crossed the room to the bed while his number two man stood in the doorway.

The first man bent down over the sleeping Tiddey and shook him roughly by the shoulder. '*Aufwachen!*' he cried in German. '*Papiere zeigen!*'

Tiddey-Oggy snored on.

The German did not hesitate. He grabbed the blanket with his free hand and pulled back. In that same instant, Tiddey-Oggy hit him full in the face with the lead-piping. The German went down as if pole-axed, his torch falling to the floor and throwing the little room into darkness.

'*Was ist –* ' the second man in the doorway began. The Toff's cruel chicken-wire noose fell over his head and lodged around his neck. The ex-public schoolboy pulled hard.

'*Aar!*' the German screamed in agony as the thin wire dug into the softness of his throat. His rifle tumbled out of suddenly nerveless fingers, which immediately began clawing at his neck to remove that killing wire. Toff leaned backwards to exert all his strength and thrust his knee into the small of the German's back, arching it as taut as a bow.

Tonsils was not idle. As Tiddey-Oggy rose, stooping only to pick up the unconscious German's machine-pistol, and started out of his bed to get the third German, Tonsils crept up behind number four. His arm crooked around the unsuspecting man's throat, catching the surprised soldier completely off guard. He drove the knife directly between his third and fourth ribs. The man gasped and weakly tried to free himself. Tonsils did not give him a chance. He withdrew his knife and thrust it home again. And again! Suddenly the German went limp. Tonsils was taking no chances. As Tiddey-Oggy felled the third German with a blow across the back of his neck, breaking it immediately and killing him before he even hit the ground, a gasping Tonsils plunged home his deadly blade one more time.

For what seemed a long time, the two men, murderer and victim, clung to each other like exhausted lovers; then Tonsils lowered the dead man to the ground, realizing suddenly that his victim was a mere boy. As he gazed down at the pale features of the dead German, whose blond hair swept across his brow in a boyish quiff, he was abruptly overcome by a feeling of remorse. For the first time in his life he had killed: a boy like himself, someone to whom he had never even spoken. He leaned across the doorjamb, his skinny body racked by sudden tears. He had killed a fellow human being!

But before this summer of 1940 was over, Patrick Mortemore, otherwise known as Tonsils, would kill many men.

SIX

Two hours later the General arrived, accompanied by his pipe-smoking ex-batman. His sharp eyes took in the three dead Germans, hidden beneath the onion sacks on the floor with only their boots protruding, and he noticed the wounded man lying on the bed breathing in harsh, shallow gasps at once. 'I see you have had visitors?' he snapped, as his ex-batman leaned over to examine the wounded man.

The three ashen-faced young Guardsmen sitting around the rickety table, drinking wine yet feeling nothing, nodded morosely. They had not yet overcome the shock of the little massacre.

The General stalked over to the shelf, reached up for a battered enamel mug, poured a measure from the bottle on the table and raised it. 'You will join me in a drink, gentlemen,' he said. It was not an invitation; it was a command. 'No heel taps,' he ordered, watching them drain their mugs before he touched his.

'You are shocked,' he continued as his gaze swept each of their faces. 'I understand it well. You are soldiers who have been in battle, but this was different, wasn't it? This was murder, you are thinking. But, gentlemen, let me tell you something: I went through the hell of Verdun in the First War and killed many men. I thought I was a hardened professional who couldn't be shaken by anything any more. But when, two years later, I escaped from the German prison camp and had to kill a frontier guard in order to cross into Switzerland, I was sick for days afterwards. Later I reasoned it was war and the enemy – whether he is at the Front or deep in his own homeland – has to be killed. Furthermore, he raised a thick manicured, if dirty, finger to emphasize his point in the French fashion – 'I – you – have a duty to kill the enemy *wherever* you find him. Let that console you, gentlemen. Now we shall have another drink and I shall tell you my news.' He gave Pierre, his ex-batman, a slight nod, knowing now that the three young Englishmen would accept what had to be done with the wounded German.

Pierre did not hesitate. He grabbed the German and flung him over his shoulder. The German groaned and, with his one arm flapping up and down along Pierre's powerful back, he allowed himself to be carried out past the three silent Englishmen. It was obvious to them all what Pierre was going to do to the teen-aged patrol-leader.

'There must be no witnesses, you understand, gentlmen,' the General said quietly as he sat down at the table. 'Now, let me tell you my news.'

'Please,' The Toff said, eager for any sound to drown out those noises which he knew must come from outside soon.

'Let me tell you the bad news first,' the General said. 'As I have already mentioned to you, a notorious *SS* battalion – which bears the title *Wotan* – is in charge of the Nîmes sector. As far as we can determine, it covers the town itself and the beaches on both sides of the port to a depth of about ten kilometres. It's a large sector, by normal military standards, but the *Wotan* is reputedly an élite organization and its commander is obviously eager for glory and promotion.' He allowed himself a sly, sideway grin. 'At all events, the *Wotan* is an alert and aggressive formation which will make it difficult for us to get to the beach.'

'What beach?' Tiddey-Oggy butted in bluntly.

'The beach from which your Royal Navy will pick us up,' the General answered blandly.

'*What?*' they exclaimed in unison.

'That is my good news,' he answered, pleased with his surprise. 'Through a good friend of mine who has still not surrendered his short-wave radio – he is a passionate radio amateur – I have made contact with your authorities in London. They have assured me that within the next two weeks, I and my friends – you – ' he spread his big hands out in an expansive gesture – 'will be taken off a suitable beach in the neighbourhood of Nîmes.'

'But how?' Tonsils asked, quicker off the mark than his comrades. 'The Jerries must have the Med bottled up, now that the Eyeties have come in on their side. The Navy wouldn't dare to send in a surface vessel to pick up you and three unimportant squaddies – soldiers to you, General – like us.'

'Possibly.' He shrugged. 'Perhaps they will send a seaplane. A submarine maybe. No matter, that is not important. The main thing is that we have the promise and that we get away from here as soon as possible.'

'You can say that again!' Tiddey-Oggy agreed in a low growl. 'After what we done tonight, we're right up the sodding creek without a sodding paddle.'

'He means, sir.' The Toff translated hurriedly for the suddenly puzzled General, 'that we are in deep waters now because of – ' He didn't finish his explanation but indicated the dead Germans with a little nod of his head.

'I agree. That was what took us so long: I had to be sure that I had found a safe house where we could be secure for the next two weeks. The search took me a long time, but in the end, I – ' He stopped short suddenly.

A long, low cry of agony penetrated the house from outside and seemed to go on endlessly until finally it was mercifully ended by a muffled blow.

The Toff felt the short hairs at the back of his head stand up. 'What was that?' he asked.

The General shrugged with Gallic eloquence but said nothing. The next moment Pierre opened the door, his face as quiet and as contained as that of a man with a clean conscience. Without a word, he went over to the corner and his big capable hands began shredding and plugging home the tobacco, without the slightest trembling.

Tonsils looked away and said, his voice not quite under control, 'General, you said that you had found a safe house for us in Nîmes – '

'Yes, indeed.' The General beamed at him for having broken the heavy silence. 'It is said, you know,' he continued

77

expansively, 'that when General Petain was called upon by the French Government of that time to rescue the nation at Verdun in nineteen-sixteen, the general who was sent to find him found him in – er – a house of ill-repute, I believe you call it in English.'

'A brothel?' Toff prompted.

'Exactly!' the General agreed. 'A brothel – and General Petain was exactly sixty years of age at that time. I am only fifty.' He grinned at the three open-mouthed young Guardsmen. 'Still, I am prepared to answer the call of France from the same place.'

'You mean . . . we're gonna hide in a knocking-shop?' Tonsils gasped.

The General nodded happily.

'*Ballocks!*' Tiddey-Oggy said in a fainting voice. 'What a way to fight a war!'

Three: The Boiling of Sgt-Major Metzger's Eggs

'Randy lot of sods – the Jerries.'
Tonsils, July 1940

ONE

As that burning June of 1940 gave way to an equally hot July, the training of *SS Assault Battalion Wotan* continued in almost murderous intensity. The days of the handful of veterans and the new recruits from the *SS* depots in the *Reich* were full of burning Mediterranean sun; the raging sea-mistral, which ripped the sun-burnt skin off their faces; hoarse, harsh orders, and frantic, back-breaking exercises which left them trembling in every limb and gasping from lungs that sounded like cracked, ancient leather bellows.

The Vulture tolerated no respite. He was everywhere, insulting the training officers in his usual cynical manner if he thought they were slack, urging on the beefy, red-faced NCOs to ever crueller efforts, slashing wildly in mad rage at the troopers if they did not meet his standards, crying crazily, the foam flying from his thin sadistic lips, 'Move faster, you hounds of hell! MOVE!'

Schulze remarked wearily to an utterly exhausted Matz, 'One day this particular hound o' hell is gonna turn round and bite the eggs off that bandy-legged little shit!'

Hounds of hell – that is what the men of *Wotan* were now becoming: lean young men with angry eyes looming out of skull-like faces, who had learned to hate with a fearsome intensity, to act without thinking at the command of a superior, and who were already dedicated to death in its most terrible form – on the field of battle.

Still The Vulture was not satisfied with the state of training of *SS Assault Battalion Wotan*. He took over the anti-tank exercises of the panzer grenadiers personally. He knew the importance of instilling in the young grenadiers the fact that a tank *could* be overcome by a determined, bold infantryman if he did not lose his head at the sight of a metal monster bearing down upon him. He knew, too, that in *Wotan*, where the tankers thought themselves the most important component of the battalion and regarded the grenadiers as stupid, big-footed, stubble-hoppers, it was vital to give the infantrymen confidence in themselves.

'You see,' he lectured the young grenadiers, most of them replacements for those who had been slaughtered in the French village, 'the tankers might think they are safely tucked away in an impregnable metal box. But if the infantryman shows courage he can turn that metal box *into a metal trap*! Let me show you what I mean.' The Vulture swung round to the two men waiting with the stirrup pumps. 'Hose the road,' he commanded in his high-pitched voice.

The two soldiers went into action, covering the cobbled French road with industrial soap until the black cobbles of the *pavé* gleamed blindingly in the hot afternoon sun.

The Vulture shrilled a blast on his whistle. Up the road, the driver of the Mark III started his engine with a roar. At forty kilometres an hour, the twenty-ton tank raced up the road and then hit the patch of soap. The driver braked violently. With a terrifying clatter of flying tracks, the tank whirled round and round, virtually out of control, it was only at the very last moment, when it seemed to the wide-eyed grenadiers that the Mark III must crash over the embankment, that the sweating, furiously cursing driver managed to bring it to a stop.

'So – ' The Vulture commented, levelling his cane at the sweat-soaked, trembling driver, 'your average tanker is *not* all-powerful after all, is he?'

His listeners were forced to agree.

Pleased with the effect of his little demonstration, The Vulture continued. He picked up one of the strange, bell-looking objects from the wooden crate at his feet and held it aloft. 'A sticky bomb,' he announced, 'which can be attached to any metal surface by means of the powerful magnets it contains. The ideal anti-tank weapon.' He walked over to the Mark III and banged the mine hard against the tank's steel side. It stuck there with a satisfying metallic clang.

'But, soldiers, where does the infantryman place such a thing?' He answered his own question. 'The bogies are out of the question: the tank will be moving when you tackle it. The front glacis plate?' Again he answered his own question. 'No, the armour is too thick there and, besides, you would undoubtedly find that the driver, the gunner and the tank commander would not exactly welcome your presence with a bomb just under their noses.' He giggled at his own attempt at humour.

There was no response from the listening grenadiers. They were too preoccupied with what was to come.

'I'm sure you have already guessed the only way to tackle a tank with a sticky bomb,' The Vulture continued. He whacked his cane down over the engine cowling to the rear of the Mark III. 'You stick it up the tank's arse. *How?* I shall show you.' He raised his voice. 'Driver, reverse and come up the road at – ah – fifteen kilometres an hour. I'll give the signal when to come.'

'Sir!'

With a clash of gears, the driver began reversing the way he had come. The Vulture stationed himself in the middle of the road, his cane tucked into his right boot, a sticky bomb held in his right hand. 'Right now!' he bellowed. '*Roll 'em!*'

The grenadiers gasped. The tank hurtled up the road directly at the CO. The distance between the two of them – man and machine – grew ever less. *One hundred metres . . . fifty . . . twenty . . .* Wasn't the Old Man ever going to jump out of the way? One moment more and the Mark III would roll over him.

Suddenly, The Vulture sprang forward. His spurs jingling loudly, he raced directly at the tank – David tackling Goliath. He grabbed at the front of the glacis plate, heaved, sprang up and over the turret and, a moment later, attached his mine to the engine cowling with a loud clang.

Hardly out of breath, he dropped off the back of the Mark III a moment later and announced simply, as if it were the most obvious thing in the world, 'Well, soldiers, and now we'll all try it – all of us. First man!' he barked, as the tank started rolling down the road once more.

The bare-headed, suddenly ashen boy breathed a swift prayer for help. Then he began running blindly, grenade clutched in his hand. In the very last moment, when it seemed he would not be able to get a grip, he managed to grab the front towing-hook and heave himself up. A second later he was lying, soaked with sweat and trembling all over, on the engine cowling, mine in place.

One by one the young grenadiers carried out the exercise, lying in the grass afterwards, shivering uncontrollably at the thought of what might have happened to them if they had failed to grab hold.

Then tragedy struck. The driver knew the kid was not going to make it. Standing there in the centre of the road, grenade held loosely in his left hand, petrified and ashen with fear, the boy was unable to move as the tank neared, filling the whole horizon with its roaring bulk. The driver, as frightened and shaken as the waiting grenadier, knew he should brake while there was still time. He knew, too, that The Vulture had expressly forbidden him to do it. 'Brake, soldier, and you'll be inside for the next four weeks! That's an order, understand?'

In the very last moment, when he knew he could not save the boy he closed his eyes and pressed his foot down hard on the clutch. There was a slight bump. Next instant the boy had disappeared under the cruel steel tracks.

The Vulture shrugged. 'An unfortunate accident,' he announced calmly as the Mark III came to a halt, squirting blood and bits of gore on the faces of the watching grenadiers. 'Next candidate.'

The brutalization of *SS Assault Battalion Wotan* continued.

The unarmed combat expert The Vulture had brought from Berlin to train the battalion was a grim-faced, plump Westphalian. It was rumoured he had once been a priest until he had been unfrocked after an *affaire* with a young novice, whereupon he had joined the Armed *SS*. At all events, it was known that in the privacy of his quarters in the NCOs' barracks he had built his own altar, complete with holy pictures and candles. 'He probably sticks them up his fat black* ass,' The Butcher commented scornfully but carefully to his closest cronies, for the ex-priest's ability with his fists and feet were feared within *Wotan* – that is, until the day came when he trained Schulze's squad.

Sergeant Xavier Joseph-Maria Bumm faced Schulze's squad, pudgy hands on pudgy hips, his chin as black as ever although he was cleanly shaven and had liberally applied talcum powder to it. 'Now then,' he remarked briskly, eyeing the young soldiers, who, aware of his reputation, avoided his gaze in case they were his first victim. 'If everyone followed the dictates of Lord Jesus Christ, there would be no evil in this world and there would be no need for evil practices such as the ones I fear I must teach you this morning.' Sergeant Bumm shrugged. 'However, as we all know – *those of us who go to church regularly, that is* – it is not a perfect world and we must be prepared to live in this imperfect universe. Therefore, today I'm going to teach you a couple of techniques which will help you to cope with the wicked ways of our fellow men.' He raised his dark eyes to heaven, as if he were making a personal apology to God for what he was being forced to do. 'First of all, I shall demonstrate to you how to ward off the common attack with a fist, though I must point out that the same technique can be used to defend oneself against a bayonet or knife attack. Now then, who is going to be first?' He beamed encouragingly at the little group of men.

Immediately their eyes fell to the ground and their hands to the front of their crotches, as if they had suddenly forgotten to put on their trousers. They all knew Sergeant Bumm's reputation. The battalion hospital was full of his victims. It was whispered about the barracks that there was

* Black is the colour of the Catholic Faith in Germany.

one father-of-three who would never be able to perform his marital duties again after a sudden encounter with Sergeant Bumm's knee.

Sergeant Bumm crossed himself quickly and pointed to a blond youth, a head taller than Corporal Schulze himself. 'You, young fellow, you'll do.'

'*Me?*' the youngster swallowed.

'Yes, you. Come on now, don't be shy.' Sergeant Bumm's benign smile vanished. 'I haven't got all day, you know. The Lord's work doesn't wait for anyone. Punch me!'

'What, Sergeant?'

'You heard me, Trooper.' There was no mistaking the threat in Bumm's voice now. His black jaw clenched and his eyes narrowed.

The blond giant clenched his fist, closed his eyes, and swung a tremendous punch at the ex-priest. The Sergeant moved at a great speed. The watching men saw something flash through the air. There was the sound of two bodies locking together. The next instant, the blond giant was lying writhing on the floor, holding his damaged testicles, while Sergeant Bumm looked down, scarcely panting, his dark eyes full of concern. 'I didn't hurt you, son, did I?' he asked. 'Not really, did I?' He bent slightly.

The shattered trooper misconstrued the gesture. '*No, no,* you didn't hurt me, Sergeant . . . But don't touch me again, *please!*'

Sergeant Bumm beamed again. 'Well, that's all right then. Now then, who's going to be next?'

Matz looked at Schulze significantly. Slowly, very slowly, Corporal Schulze closed his right eye.

One by one Sergeant Bumm took on the whole squad, some armed with a bayonet, some with a knife. One by one he laid them on their backs, writhing in the grass, battered and bruised, holding their injured crotches. Halfway through the exercise, he paused and asked, 'Now, who of you are Catholics?'

When no one answered, he said mildly, 'But surely some of you men must be Catholic?'

When no one responded, he said, 'All right, probably

you're shy. Who of you are from Bavaria or Westphalia then?'

A few hands shot up.

'Good.' He smiled at the men with the raised hands. 'Now, those two provinces are nearly one hundred per cent Catholic, so you men must be Catholic.' He bent suddenly on one knee. 'You and I shall say a *Hail Mary* together before we proceed any further.' He closed his eyes and folded his hands reverently and began the prayer.

'Holy strawsack,' Matz whispered. 'The sod has just ruined half these lads' sex life for ever and now he's on a private call to the Big Rain-Maker himself! What a shitting hypocrite!'

'Wrong you ain't, Matzi,' Schulze agreed. 'He gives me a pain in the pisser. I think the time has come for Sergeant Bumm to meet his Maker.'

Finished with his prayer, Sergeant Bumm rose to his feet again and beamed at the squad. 'Now, who's left?' he demanded. 'Don't be shy or fearful. After all, it is the work of the Lord that I am doing, helping you to cope with an evil world.'

Hesitantly Corporal Schulze raised his hand. 'I don't think I've had a go yet, Sergeant,' he said in his meekest voice. 'I hope I'm not being too forward, Sergeant,' he added, lowering his head, as if in embarrassment.

'Of course not, Corporal,' the NCO answered, full of fake joviality. 'Come on, old chap, hit me with your fist.'

'Oh, I couldn't do that.'

'Come now, try,' Sergeant Bumm said encouragingly, 'though I can't guarantee you'll be able to hit me. Ha, ha!' He began to laugh at his own humour in the very same instant that Schulze launched himself forward.

Bumm reacted quickly enough to the surprise attack, blocking the tremendous haymaker that Schulze launched at his head. But the big ex-docker had not survived on Hamburg's tough waterfront for so long by playing the game according to the rules. As he launched a punch at the Sergeant's head, his big dice-beaker came up and slammed directly into the NCO's crotch. Bumm flew back, screaming, his false teeth bulging out of his gaping mouth absurdly as he hit the ground, writing in agony.

Solemnly Schulze bent on one knee next to the stricken NCO, blessed him carefully and then, winking at his sorely tried squad, said in solemn tones, 'Comrades, shall we pray . . .'

The harsh training exercises continued night and day. Practice bombs were tossed through the open windows of the barracks in the early morning and followed by the harsh cries of the NCOs: 'All right, you bunch of greenbeaks, you're dead if you're not out of those bunks within five seconds. *At the double!*'

The sudden burst of machine-gun fire that chipped fragments off the ancient stone buildings as the weary troopers lined up to receive their midday meal was accompanied by the shrill whistles and frantic whirls of the wooden rattles. 'Air-raid . . . air-raid. *Everybody down!*' The excited hash-slingers overturned the horsemeat soup, flooding the courtyard with greasy thick swill so that the exhausted soldiers screamed with the sudden pain.

Breasting the high waves in full equipment, the non-swimmers fought furiously to keep their feet as the waves swept over them and dragged them down to the screams of those who were carried out to sea for ever.

'Why?' von Dodenburg asked The Vulture during a quiet moment in the officers' casino that month.

'Why?' The Vulture echoed increduously. 'What else is there for a soldier to do? You should know that, von Dodenburg; you are a regular, not one of your typical *SS* asphalt soldiers either,' he added with a sneer.

Von Dodenburg accepted the comment; it was typical of the pre-war Regular Army, to which The Vulture had belonged. He and his kind had always believed the *SS* was only good enough to goose-step over Berlin's asphalt-covered streets in ceremonial parades for the Führer and the Party *prominenz*.

'We train,' The Vulture continued, 'to die a little bit later than if we didn't.'

'But the war is over. We are at peace once more.'

'And the Tommies?' The Vulture asked.

'Everyone knows they are finished. They ran away at Dunkirk. Their Army is a weaponless rabble now. It is over a month since they abandoned the continent, and they have taken no offensive action whatsoever, sir – unless you regard that blustering and sabre-rattling of Churchill's as offensive action?'

The Vulture put down his glass of champagne slowly. 'Von Dodenburg, do you really think that the greatest empire the world has ever seen would allow an undersized, ex-Austrian lance-corporal with a funny moustache named Hitler to get away with the rape of western Europe? Do you?' He grinned cynically. 'No, my dear young friend. The Tommies will be back, somewhere or other, sooner or later. It is for that reason that we must train, train, train! After all, I am still not a general like my father and his father before him. With a bit of luck the Tommies will help me to obtain my general's stars yet. Oh, yes, von Dodenburg, rest assured – the Tommies will be back . . .'

Just how soon they would rejoin the fray, the bandy-legged, beak-nosed major could not have guessed then.

TWO

C stepped out of the ancient Rolls and placed his bowler more firmly on his thinning hair. Above him a group of Spitfires and Messerschmidts were engaged in a snarling, howling dog-fight, with their machine-guns chattering frantically. C hardly noticed; he was too preoccupied with what he had to say to Symbole.

The middle-aged doorman of the Connaught Hotel, wearing a tin hat instead of his usual topper, opened the door and grinned at the pale-faced, pale-eyed Head of the British Secret Service. 'We've really got them on a sticky wicket today, sir,' he said happily, indicating the sky.

'What's the score?' C asked, feeling a fool as he did so. This month everyone talked as if the life-or-death struggle being fought out in the sky above London was some kind of murderous cricket match.

'A hundred of theirs for twenty of ours. Not a bad average, sir, eh?'

'Not bad at all,' C agreed. 'Now I would be pleased if you could tell me where the – er – French gentleman is? I am expected.'

The doorman clicked his fingers. An ancient porter, as padded and as worn as the thick carpets of the old-fashioned hotel, came over and led C to a drawing-room, where a table for two was already laid.

The officer in the uniform of the Free French Army, standing at the window, with its panes criss-crossed with sticky tape to prevent the glass from being blown out by the blast, swung round. Viewing the man's pale, red-rimmed eyes and rather porcine features, C took an immediate dislike to the Frenchman.

'Colonel Menzies, I presume?' the officer said in good English.

'Colonel Bourse,' C replied, knowing he was facing the head of Symbole's secret service.

They shook hands. For a moment or two there was an awkward silence while the two of them tried to sum each other up – and failed; they were both experts in not revealing their true feelings. Finally Bourse asked, 'Have your people decided, Colonel?'

C nodded.

Bourse frowned. 'Symbole won't like it. He regards himself as the sole guardian of the flame of French resistance outside France. You know that he has sacrificed all to come to London and continue the struggle. Do you know yesterday he had a letter returned from General Weygand* with these words scribbled across it: 'If retired Colonel – '

He stopped short. Symbole had entered the room. He waved a rather feminine hand attached to a too-slender wrist. Colonel Bourse went out without another word.

'*Enchante, M'sieu*,' Symbole said and took C's outstretched hand. He gave it a limp shake and then indicated that the Head of the Secret Service should take a seat. A moment later an aged waiter brought in the soup. They ate in silence, while they studied each other.

C found Symbole taller than he expected. His movements were slow and heavy, like his huge nose, which seemed out of place in such a small, waxen face. For a Frenchman he used few gestures, but he had a habitual one: he raised his very white, feminine hands, palms outwards and downwards, as if he were raising the burden of the whole world on them. To C, the gesture seemed significant. Symbole obviously did feel it was his responsibility to bear a heavy burden. Did he see himself, this obscure Frenchman, as a leader of a future free France, he wondered?

The main course came – a poor piece of meat, plus de-hydrated potatoes – and Symbole voiced the reason for this

---

* Head of the French Army in France.

meeting at his hotel headquarters. 'You recall, *mon Colonel*, that when I spoke to my people last June, I told them the war is not limited to our unfortunate country. The outcome of the struggle has not been decided by the Battle of France. I then concluded by calling on all French officers and men presently on British soil to contact me and continue the struggle. By doing that, I achieved two things. I have rallied that part of France to me that still wants to fight. Secondly, I have burnt my boats behind me. I stand, in the eyes of many in France, as a traitor. If I returned to my homeland now, undoubtedly there would be those in the Army who would ensure that I were court-martialed, possibly shot for high treason. You understand?'

C understood, but he understood more than Symbole intended. The man facing him did not love his fellow Frenchmen; he loved their history, *la gloire*. Now he wanted to write a chapter recording his own deeds. In this dark, old-fashioned dining-room, with the snarl of the aerial battle taking place over their heads penetrating from outside, he was making his play for a place in the annals of *la grande nation*.

Symbole finished the last of the mashed potatoes with a slight shudder and continued. 'I have, therefore, sacrificed all to carry on the struggle in the English camp. Now I hear rumours that you intend to bring Gilles to England, too.' His long nose twitched disdainfully. 'What is he, eh?' He raised his forearms, elbows tight to his side, like an angry duck flapping its wings. 'A broken-down infantryman, nearly ten years older than I, who admittedly had some success in the battle for my poor country. But I had success, too, with my Fourth Armoured Division, and I am, modesty aside, my country's foremost expert on modern warfare. He, Gilles, is still fighting the First War.'

Patiently C waited till the Frenchman had finished, his cold eyes revealing nothing. For nearly four years on Haig's staff in the first show, he had dealt with the French. He knew them well. Beneath their Gallic gestures and posture, they were cold, calculating realists, much more so than the, supposedly, dry English.

'Everything you have said, sir, is correct,' he began carefully. 'But I must point out that General Gilles is a senior, full general, while your rank is . . .' he left the point unfinished, then continued. 'Moreover, because of his many years in North Africa he has the loyalty of the Colonial Army. By our estimates, that Army consists of some half-million men. They would be a considerable addition to our strength, especially if we could convince the fleet at Oran to come over to us. General Gilles is probably the best placed Frenchman to achieve that important aim.'

Symbole looked at him coldly, the batter pudding which the waiter had just brought him growing cold on the plate in front of him. 'You have already made your decision, haven't you?'

C nodded, expecting an outburst.

Instead, Symbole asked, 'When and where?'

'The Prime Minister Mr Churchill has given my organization the task of fetching General Gilles – '

'When and where?' Symbole interrupted him brutally, his anger showing through now.

'When, we don't know exactly. We are having difficulty with the Royal Navy in obtaining the necessary submarine to pull him out. Where is easier – Nîmes on the Mediterranean coast. The sector is only lightly guarded by one *SS* battalion.'

'I see,' Symbole said, calm again. He rose to his feet and stretched himself to his full height, towering above the pale-faced secret service man. 'You realize that I am in your hands completely. The die has been cast.' His dark eyes glowered. 'But I will not forget this, Colonel. *Never!*' He dropped his napkin on the table.

Colonel Menzies understood the gesture. It was time to go. He departed without shaking hands, telling himself he must get that damned sub out of the Navy soon; the man was a monomaniac.

Symbole waited till the Englishman's ancient Rolls had drawn away, and then he strode from the window and rang the bell. Bourse appeared at once, as if he had been listening at the door all the time, waiting for this summons.

'Well?'

93

'They are bringing him to England.'

'*Sales cons!*' Bourse cursed, unable to keep his temper under control.

Symbole shrugged. 'So, it is a fact and we must face up to it. What do we do, Bourse?'

His Chief-of-Intelligence looked at Symbole, puzzled. 'How do you mean, sir? What can we do? What is that Racine says? *Sans argent, l'honneur n'est qu'une maladie.** We are completely in the Britishers' hands. We have no money and barely any power. They act, we accept.'

The giant shook his head firmly. 'No, Bourse. They act and we react. I will not tolerate Gilles being brought to this country after what I have sacrificed for the British cause.'

Bourse looked at him, aghast. He knew Symbole of old, but he did not think he would go *that* far. 'You don't mean, sir, *stop him*?'

'I do.'

There was a tremendous crash from outside and the windows rattled violently as a fighter plunged to its doom in central London. Symbole waited till the noise had ceased, his waxen face showing neither fear nor joy. 'I do not want to know the nasty details, Colonel Bourse, but I am now giving you a direct order. You are to stop General Gilles leaving Nîmes. Is that clear?'

'Clear, sir.'

'Good. Go and set about the task at once.'

Bourse left, leaving the waxen-faced giant who had once been known as General de Gaulle but who now covered up his identity in this run-down hotel under the codename Symbole, staring broodingly into a grey future . . .

* Without money, honour is nothing but a disease.

94

THREE

'Randy lot of sods – the Jerries,' Tonsils commented as they peered out of the attic window at the long lines of excited young men in field-grey and the black of the armoured troops queueing up noisily outside the brothel.

'Listen who's talking,' Tiddey-Oggy said sourly. 'You got yer share last night after the shop closed for the night.'

Tonsils looked at his nails with mock modesty. 'Some of us have it and others ain't,' he said.

'Ballocks!'

Tonsils said, 'I'll give yer a recipe, mate – stew in your own juice.'

The Toff smiled. They had been hiding in the brothel nearly a week now and in spite of the fact that the three young men were getting more sex than they had ever had before – the girls, it seemed, couldn't do enough for them – the narrow confines of their hiding place were beginning to get on all their nerves. Also, the uncertainty of their future was getting them down.

'That little blonde – Marie – with the big tits, she really goes a bundle on me,' Tonsils continued. 'Do you know what she did to me last night?'

Below, a great roar that went up as the girls arrived back from their afternoon walk ready for business, drowned the rest of his words. The excited young soldiers in the queue started to shove and push, and the German military policemen at the door were forced to use their carbines to press the soldiers back in order to let the girls through. Giggling and squealing, they ran the gauntlet of the German soldiers, who attempted to kiss them and pinch their plump behinds, while to the rear the owner of the brothel, Madame Broglie, her enormous bosom threatening to burst out of her black silk blouse at any moment, waved her sunshade and yelled, 'Get off, you pigs . . . Get off or I'll put you on my black list . . . *Get off!*'

The Toff sat down, grinning. 'Some character, that Madame,' he said.

Tonsils sat down next to him on the hard wooden bench near the window. 'She looks to me as if she's had more screws than good dinners.'

'Yer right there,' Tiddey-Oggy agreed. 'Do you think the old General gives it to her? He's holed up with her most nights when the shop closes up, ain't he?'

'No, gentlemen, I am afraid I have not had that particular pleasure yet.'

It was the General himself, standing grinning at the door of the attic. Hurriedly the three men rose to their feet and snapped to attention, Tiddey-Oggy red in the face with embarrassment.

'Sorry sir,' The Toff said quickly. 'We didn't mean it like that. It's this place – '

Good-humouredly the General waved them to stand at ease. 'Think nothing of it, my dear chap. If I were your age and living in this – er – establishment, I am sure I would be thinking of nothing else but that. Please be seated. I have something to discuss with you.'

They took a seat on the bench, sitting there like overgrown schoolboys, General Gilles could not help thinking. For a moment his heart went out to them, and he promised himself that, however impossible, he would get them back to their own country. Sitting down on the one chair, he dug into the pocket of his shabby civilian jacket and brought out the two packets of cigarettes he had bought for them on the black market. He tossed them to the red-haired youth, who was the heaviest smoker, and said: 'Gentlemen, I have received the news I have been waiting for. Your fellow countrymen are sending a submarine to fetch us.'

The Englishmen's faces lit up. Even Tiddey-Oggy's usual gloomy expression disappeared.

'I say, sir,' The Toff breathed enthusiastically, 'that really is good news! When?'

'I have been informed that the submarine will take up its position on the coast to the south of Nîmes on two nights in the middle of next week.'

'Middle of the week,' Tonsils cried. 'Did yer hear that, lads? Next week we're off back to Blighty!'

'Crikey, I'll be able to eat a bit o' decent grub again, instead of this French muck,' the Portsmouth man exclaimed.

'Tiddey-Oggy, naturally,' The Toff and Tonsils said in unison.

'And why not?' Tiddey-Oggy grumbled. 'That's real grub!'

'Gentlemen,' General Gilles commanded, and they fell silent at once. 'Let me put you in the picture. In July the citizens of Nîmes celebrate their annual festival. We are not far from Spain here, you know, and the townspeople hold bull-fights and the like in the old Roman arena.' He shrugged a little helplessly. 'The fact that we have lost the war does not seem to worry the people here. They must have their bread and circuses - it is the nature of the Frenchman of the south. All attention will be concentrated on the festival, and the Boche have gone so far as to allow the curfew to be lifted for those two days. In other words, we can circulate as we wish after dark. You understand?'

They nodded.

'Good. Our problem is how to secure a stretch of beach long enough for the submarine to land a dinghy and pick us up. It might sound easy to you. The beach here is large enough – ten kilometres at least to the south of the town, I should estimate – but my people tell me that the Boche have stepped up their patrols. They are out every night, and there is no reason to expect they won't be out on those two nights next week.'

'We've got the weapons we took off the Jerries, sir,' The Toff said stoutly. 'We could make a fight for it.'

The General smiled. 'I have no doubt about that,' he said. 'But, my young friend, what do you think would be the reaction of the submarine's captain if he heard firing going on on the beach? I can tell you. Naval captains place their vessel first. He would submerge at once and make a run for it, leaving us in a decidedly unpleasant position.'

Tiddey-Oggy nodded his agreement. 'In the Royal Navy, the ship always comes first. My dad always said that.'

'No, the General continued, 'we must slip on to the beach between patrols and get away without any fighting. This is what I propose . . .'

The Englishmen listened attentively while the General outlined his bold plan. When he was finished, The Toff said, 'Well, sir, at least it is very original.'

'I think so,' the Frenchman replied.

'But do you think the Madame will go along with it?' Tonsils asked. 'I mean, it's dangerous.'

'Of course, that is why I have been closeted with her so often of late. I was sounding her out, not doing what your pornographic fantasy imagined. No, Madame Broglie might be a whore, but she is also a French patriot. She'll go along with my proposal, I am sure of that.' He rose. 'Gentlemen, I must be gone. There is still a lot to be done.' He winked at them solemnly. 'I beg you save a little of your strength. We will have need of it in the week to come.'

Tonsils laughed and said, 'General, but isn't it a lovely way to go, eh?'

The General laughed, too, and because of it he did not catch the glint of glass from the window of the empty house opposite. It was to be an unfortunate oversight.

Agnelli lowered his binoculars and cursed himself for not having been more careful. He should have protected the lenses against the slanting rays of the afternoon sun with his hand.

'Well,' asked Jo-Jo Bastian, crouching next to him in the dusty, bare room. 'It is the pig?'

'I think so, Jo-Jo.'

'The bastard! He approved the five-year rap I took in Africa in thirty-six just because I spat in the face of the drill instructor. Five long shitty years for a bit of spit – and they call that French justice.' He rubbed a grimy hand the size of a small shovel across his heavy unshaven jaw. 'I'd like to pay him back for that.'

'You will,' Agnelli answered slowly and reflectively. He was a small, swarthy, sharp-featured man with a livid knife-scar running right down the left side of his face, a souvenir of his days as a pimp in Marseilles. Now fate had made him chief of de Gaulle's intelligence service in the Provence. He was determined to carry out his first important assignment from London correctly, for he had already reasoned that London could mean money – a lot of money. He turned to face his companion.

Jo-Jo, big, lumbering and slow-thinking as he was, was the ideal man for the job. He hated Gilles, and the ex-docker, who found his new activity a more profitable venture than lugging sacks of cement on the docks, was not a man to mince matters. He had a bad reputation as a bully and brawler.

'Now, Jo-Jo,' he said slowly and carefully, as if he were talking to a very small child, 'I want you to follow Gilles everywhere he goes from now on. I want to know everyone he meets and everything he does. Clear?'

'Clear,' Jo-Jo growled, idly picking his nose with a fore-finger as thick as a sausage. 'You don't want to let me lay a cold flipper on him, but I'd like to pay him back for Africa!'

'No, Jo-Jo,' Agnelli said firmly. 'Just follow him. No one is to know about us or know that we have any connection with Gilles. Do you understand? When the time comes, we'll let the Boche take care of *Monsieur le General Gilles*.'

Jo-Jo looked at the sharp-faced ex-pimp stupidly. 'You don't mean – '

'I do,' Agnelli replied coldly. 'Then we'll betray him to the Fritzes. Who knows – ' he shrugged unfeelingly – 'perhaps we might make a little dough out of the deal. All right, Jo-Jo, be off with you – and watch out for that little bastard with the pipe who's waiting for him downstairs at Broglie's. He looks a sly one. Don't let him spot you.'

'I won't, Agnelli, I promise. *Ciaou*.'

'*Ciaou*,' Agnelli echoed, amused by the fact that the big oaf, who couldn't speak his own language correctly, used an Italian word.

Five minutes later he was gone himself, slinking in the shadows of the back-street like the ally rat he was.

FOUR

The men of De Gaulle's intelligence service were not the only ones who were interested in the goings-on at Madame Broglie's waterfront brothel. Corporal Schulze, in the furtherance of his plan to wreak a terrible revenge on Sergeant-Major Metzger, had also been studying the place and its occupants carefully ever since the episode with The Vulture's thunderbox.

As he explained to Matz, 'The sod's got it coming to him. If we don't put him down now, once and for all, the big bastard of a pork butcher will make our lives hell until the Führer, in his infinite wisdom, decides to give the *SS* a break and release us from service.'

'I thought you were a regular.'

'Yes, but only in the crapper. Now listen, and don't get side-tracked. You know The Butcher's taste in women, don't yer?'

'Yer, the three-B type: bust, belly and behind – and plenty of all three.'

'Exactly. I've found just the type for him in that brothel I was telling you about. A little blonde called Marie, with plenty of wood in front of the door.' His big hands shaped what looked like two small barrage ballons in the air.

Matz was unimpressed. 'What gives with you, Schulze? You ain't turned brown-noser or something, have yer, trying to find dames for The Butcher.'

'Of course not, stupid!' Schulze snorted. 'It's part of my plan.'

'What plan?'

'The plan to shaft The Butcher so hard that he won't be

able to sit down again for a month o' Sundays.'

'Well, how does this Marie fit into it?'

'Because, birdbrain, dummies like The Butcher think Frog tarts are the best in the world. It's something they've read in the dirty books they hide beneath their pillows. Wanker's doom – here I come, I don't want to be a pilot after all, sir and all that. You know?'

'I don't,' Matz said solemnly. 'I go to church regularly every Saturday morning and try to keep myself clean for a nice Jewish girl.'

'Arse with ears,' Schulze cursed. 'Now listen. Well, Frog tarts are what he's after – and he ain't having much luck with The Vulture trying to stop the men from going to the knocking-shops with night exercises, patrols and all the rest of it. However, through a third party, I have let our beloved Sergeant-Major know that there is a certain Marie who has the very definite hots for him.'

'Well, they say rape is assault with a friendly weapon,' Matz commented, apropos of nothing.

'Shut up and listen! This afternoon our beloved Sergeant-Major is going to pay a visit to Marie, and he's gonna get the surprise of his life.'

'How do you mean?' Matz asked, taking in the malicious look of anticipation in his running-mate's eyes.

'All I'm saying at this moment is that Sergeant-Major Metzger is going to get more French loving than he ever bargained for.' He chuckled throatily. 'Shouldn't be surprised if she doesn't have the eggs off'n him this afternoon – and it couldn't happen to a nicer feller.'

'How right you are, Schulze. Let us have one minute of silent prayer for the loss of Sergeant-Major Metzger's eggs. Amen.'

'*A-men . . .*'

'Oh-la-la!' Marie squealed in apparent delight as she took Sergeant-Major Metzger's sexual organ in her hands and felt it, as if she were trying to guess its weight.

'It's all there, *cherie*,' The Butcher said proudly. He gave a coarse chuckle and slapped the whore's plump naked behind. 'I wasn't about to leave any at the barracks *this* day.'

Marie pressed it down and let it spring up of its own accord – again. 'It marches,' she simpered in fractured German.

'Of course it does,' The Butcher answered delightedly. 'That thing's got a mind of its own, you know.' He leaned back with a sigh of pleasure and let her commence the usual routine of washing his apparatus with warm water and soap. She whistled *Wir fahren gegen England** softly as she did so.

Carefully and gently she dried The Butcher with a small towel, and for a moment it was suspended above his hairy, fat stomach as if on a flagpole.

'Good, good,' she said in approval.

'You bet it's good. Prime quality German beef, that – you fancy a bite of it?' He reached out to grab her, but she avoided his grasp and crossed over to the hot plate on which she had warmed the water. She refilled the pot from the tap in the corner and placed it on the dull red plate.

'You wait one little moment, *cherie*,' she announced, swinging round, her breasts flying up with the motion as if they might sail away into space at any moment. 'Then we make love – *à la française*.'

'I don't know what that Frog means,' Metzger bellowed happily, 'but if it's dirty, I'm all for it!'

The pan of water was boiling merrily on the glowing plate. Marie tested it with her finger and gave a little yelp of pain. It was very hot. She beckoned seductively at the naked NCO. 'Come, my little rabbit, now you get it.'

Metzger lumbered to his feet. Like a lamb being led to the slaughter, he allowed her to lead him over to the bubbling pot. 'What's this?' he demanded happily, his big paws mauling her massive breasts. 'What are you going to show a good honest soldier first?'

'You bend - *comme ça*.' She bent, legs spread wide apart over the pot, to indicate what she meant.

'Bend?' he asked, his low brow creased with bewilderment.

* *We march against England*, a favourite SS marching song of 1940.

103

'That water looks shitting hot to me.'

'Good, good,' she said encouragingly and pulled the flagpole he was bearing in front of him a couple of times. 'You like? You never had anything like it before.'

'Like leprosy,' he chortled, using the old soldier's crack, and bent over the bubbling pot. 'Tell me when they're nice, crisp and brown. Ha, ha!'

'Ha, ha!' she agreed, smiling. 'Lower, my little rabbit, lower!'

Sergeant-Major Metzger felt the heat begin to stir his already overheated loins, but his curiosity got the better of him. It would be a good tale to tell his cronies in the mess. His knees creaking, he bent lower, sweat standing out in great beads on his crimson face.

'*Bon, bon,*' she urged, thrusting one huge, brown-nippled breast in his face. 'Lower!'

He bent lower. He nearly cried out from the heat tearing at his genitals, but he pulled himself together. He must soldier on. He bit his bottom lip to control the cry of pain. What did she have in mind for him? It must be something special for her to be toasting his eggs like this. Now the sweat was pouring from his gross body in great rivulets.

'A little lower – just a little lower,' she hissed, her tongue thrust deep into his ear. 'And then – then you get it.'

'If you say so,' he groaned, feeling the burning heat rip at him. 'But it better be good – ' His words ended in a howl of pain, as his sexual organ disappeared into the boiling hot water. Like a vengeful sword, pain sliced into his lower body. He jumped up, crying, 'You've burnt 'em off me! You've burnt my eggs off'n me. *I'm ruined!*'

While Marie stood racked with laughter, the tears running down her berouged face, he hopped up and down in agony, dancing from one foot to the other, his lower body crab-red. He attempted to double up and blow cool air on his tortured genitals and, in the end, realized that a tap was there. He rushed over and turned it on full stream, breathing out a great sigh of relief as the cold water flooded over his injured organ, sending up a cloud of hissing steam.

In the centre of the room, Marie, comforted by the

knowledge that the other funny German had paid her two pounds of coffee and a carton of black market cigarettes to play this strange trick on his comrade, laughed and laughed and laughed . . .

'Sergeant-Major,' the sentry said urgently.

'Don't bother me,' The Butcher groaned, as he stood at the gate to the barracks, bow-legged, with his hands holding his injured genitals carefully. 'Let me die in peace.' He attempted to brush the earnest, young sentry to one side.

'But the CO said specifically that I must stop you at the gate, sir.'

'Screw you, the CO and the whole of France,' The Butcher moaned. 'I want to get to my bunk.'

'But, sir – '

'*Sergeant-Major!*' An all-too familiar high-pitched voice rent the air.

Sergeant-Major Metzger's heart sank. It was The Vulture. 'Sir?' he answered in a fainting voice.

'Over here – *at the double!*'

The Butcher started to shamble over to where a red-faced, obviously angry Vulture stood, tapping his cane impatiently against the side of his highly polished riding boot.

'*At the double*, I said, Sergeant-Major!'

Groaning inwardly, The Butcher doubled the best he could towards the CO.

'Where have you been, man?' The Vulture exploded. 'I've been looking for you everywhere in the barracks. No matter. Look at this piggery, will you?' With his cane, he flicked back the canvas that was spread out at his booted feet.

Four waxen faces came into view, one of them with a bullet hole drilled neatly through the head. 'The missing patrol,' The Vulture announced icily. 'I thought the green-beaks had deserted. And so they had, in a way – for good. They have been murdered.'

'What . . . what?' The Butcher stuttered, holding on tightly to his injured organ, as the CO flicked at the middle man's throat with his cane. 'That one was strangled with what appears to have been chicken wire. The next one was stabbed. The third one was killed by a blunt instrument.' He turned the corpse's face so that The Butcher could see the livid bruise which disfigured the youth's temple. 'And this one was shot very neatly through the temple. What do you make of that, eh, Sergeant-Major Metzger?'

'It looks like – ' Metzger began.

The Vulture did not allow him to finish. 'I'll tell you what it looks like, Sergeant-Major. It looks like cold-blooded murder to me. My poor troopers were lured into a trap and then slaughtered like poor dumb animals.' He thrashed his cane through the air in anger. 'I'm not having it, Sergeant-Major! Nobody is going to get away with that kind of nastiness in my sector. *SS Assault Battalion Wotan* is not to be stabbed in the back by some damned alley-rat of a Frenchman!'

'What do you expect me to do, sir?'

'*Expect* you to do!' The Vulture exploded. 'I'll tell you what I *expect* you to do, Sergeant-Major. I *expect* you to get my men out of those damned swinish brothels and cafés where they sit guzzling wine and beer and have them on patrol night and day until they find the pigs who killed these chaps here. I *expect* you – ' he pointed his cane directly at Metzger, his hand trembling with rage – 'to find the criminals, or by God and Adolf Hitler, you'd better apply for a transfer to the quartermaster's branch.'

With that he stalked away, leaving an unfortunate Sergeant-Major Metzger holding his burning genitals and wishing he had never left the *Reich* . . .

Four: The Plan

'It is vital for this country that you pick up General Gilles.'
C to Lt-Commander Higgs, July 1940

ONE

Watery darkness lapped against the black hull of the submarine. Sailors were busy removing the guard rail. Once they were at sea they would not need it. On the bridge the men on watch shifted about silently, looking now and again at the searchlights which poked icy-white fingers into the blackness over the port.

C reached into the pocket of his British Warm and brought out the little silver flask. 'It is a custom of our service, Commander,' he said to the tall, boyish submarine skipper who had a silk scarf thrown over his shoulder carelessly. 'We always give a flask of brandy or whisky to our chaps when they go off on a mission.'

Lieutenant-Commander Higgs, known throughout the service as Piggs, accepted the flask with a smile. 'To speed the hasty hero to his death *happily*, I presume, Colonel.'

C frowned. Already in this war he had sent enough brave young men to their deaths; he did nót like to joke about such things. 'Let us not talk about that,' he said severely. 'I'll repeat my orders. It is vital for this country that you pick up General Gilles, but – and I emphasize the *but* – you are not to risk your ship and your crew to do so. You understand, Commander?'

'Of course, Colonel. I don't take the responsibility of looking after the lives of forty-odd chaps lightly. But they are good fellows. They've run risks before and they'll run them again.'

'I'm glad to hear that,' C said. 'You do understand that the Boche have got the Med virtually tied up, now that the Iagoes have come in on their side. Once you're past Gib, the Boche or their allies will be watching out for you all the way. They've got their people permanently stationed at Algericas, opposite Gib – within spitting distance, if you'll forgive the phrase – and they report everything that goes into the Med to their Naval High Command.'

The Commander's grin vanished. 'We'll go in under the cover of darkness and submerged. I think we'll make it.' He thrust out his hand. 'Well, Colonel, we must run out while we've still got darkness. They're very strict about security here, just in case Jerry has his agents stationed here in port.'

C took the hand and pressed it hard, somewhat moved. He knew the risk the submarine skipper was running. 'Happy landings,' he said, using a phrase from another war.

Higgs grinned again. 'Happy landings it is, sir. And thank you.'

'Start all main engines!'

The bosun jerked back all the levers to ALL BACK ONE-THIRD. Slowly HMS *Swordfish* started to move away from the pier.

Lieutenant-Commander Higgs muttered another order into the tube.

The bosun, his brawny arms covered with fading tattoos up to the shoulder, shoved the levers to ALL AHEAD ONE-THIRD. The lean submarine started to pick up speed.

On the bridge, Higgs felt the breeze begin to ruffle his long hair. He put on his battered white cap, its gold braid long ago tarnished green by the salt. He licked suddenly dry lips and felt once again the excitement that a year of wartime missions like this had not killed. 'Clear the bridge!' he commanded, his voice full of urgency. '*DIVE . . . DIVE!*'

The sirens sounded. The deck watch tumbled down the hatch. Higgs followed. Inside the submarine, the green and red lights started to flash urgently. Slowly HMS *Swordfish* began to submerge.

The rescue operation was underway . . .

TWO

'Well, you arse with ears,' Matz said lazily. 'what now?'

'What now?' Schulze repeated, giving a long contented fart as he lay in the hot sand. 'I'm going to lie here and think myself randy.' He stretched out with a sigh of relief, helmet, machine-pistol and pack spread out next to him.

'May I remind the Mister Corporal that we are supposed to be on patrol, looking for those Frog bastards who did for our lads?' Matz said, looking at the youngsters who were staring at the two of them as if they had landed from the moon. 'Those wet-tails take this kind of thing serious, you know.'

Schulze raised one fat forefinger. 'Sit on it,' he said lazily. 'You, too!'

'And your mother,' Schulze said, continuing the old routine.

'Your grandmother as well.'

'She can't. It's all dried up.'

'Oh come on, Schulze,' Matz persisted, 'you know The Vulture. If he finds you hitting the hay like that, he'll have the knackers off you.'

'What am I supposed to do?' Schulze said grumpily.

'Get the lead out of your butt and patrol – or, at least, pretend to patrol, you asparagus Tarzan.'

Matz held out his hand. 'Here, grab the flipper and raise your brittle bones,' he ordered.

With a groan, Schulze did as commanded. 'What's up with you, Matzi?' he asked, putting on his helmet again. 'You bucking for promotion or something? Don't you know the big war is over. War is hell – '

'And peacetime'll kill you.' Matz beat him to it. 'Now move it!'

Schulze waved a lazy paw at the round-eyed, teen-aged grenadiers. 'All right, girls. Don't just stand around. You heard Trained Soldier Matz – move those brittle bones.'

The 'girls' grinned and started to trail along behind the big corporal, who carried his machine-pistol in one big hand as if it were a child's toy.

Half an hour passed. The going was tough as they ploughed through the deep sand under a hot July sun. All of them were lathered in sweat, their uniforms black with perspiration. Doggedly they slogged on, the only sound being their own heavy breathing and the occasional metallic clank of their equipment. To their left the sea was a brilliant blue, giving off a glare that hurt their eyes. To their right was the dead-straight road, completely empty and bordered here and there by tangles of bramble and briar. The Vulture had ordered it closed to all French civilians after the murder of the patrol.

Schulze, in the lead, was preoccupied with his own thoughts. Lulled by the silence and the burning heat, his mind was savouring the probable pleasures of this night's visit to Madam Broglie, where he was now a regular, well-liked customer. For this reason he did not see the sudden glint of glass from the clump of bramble bushes a hundred metres to their right. His first indication that the beach was not deserted was the sharp, dry crack of a rifle.

Directly behind him, the young bare-headed trooper paused in mid-stride, a bewildered look on his face. A moment later he pitched forward into the sand, *dead*.

'Take cover!' Schulze bellowed, flinging himself full-length as the rifle cracked once more.

The patrol scattered swiftly. Matz, bringing up the rear, hosed the bushes to their right with his machine-pistol, until a hasty spurt of sand a metre away from him warned him that the unknown sniper was zeroing in on him. Then, he too, dived for cover.

Schulze bent his head as another slug hissed above and did some quick thinking. The sniper – or snipers – had picked a perfect position. The beach was absolutely without cover. They were pinned down, and the only way that they were going to survive was to keep their snouts buried in the hot sand. But Schulze knew, too, that he could not allow his patrol to be trapped like this. He had to do something.

He flashed a look to the right and ducked just in time as another slug howled by him. That was it: the only way. The attackers would not expect this course of action. He eased off his helmet and pack. 'Matz,' he yelled, 'give me covering fire.'

'What?'

'You heard – I'm gonna take off. *NOW!*'

In a flash, he was up on his feet, machine-pistol slung over his shoulder, and began pelting towards the sea. The sniper realized too late that he was running away. A volley of slugs stitched a crazy pattern at Schulze's flying feet. A second later, Schulze took a flat dive into the water and was swimming underwater out of range.

Gasping for breath, his broad chest heaving with the strain, Schulze pulled himself out of the water and lay full-length in the wet sand for a moment. He had done it. He had come up behind the snipers, who were now hidden from sight behind the clump of bushes. He breathed in deeply and then started to crawl forward, machine-pistol thrust in front of him, working his way up the beach on his belly. Any noise he might have made was covered up by the crackle of musketry.

Then he was in position. Cautiously, he poked his head over the sand hillock and stared down at the civilians crouched behind the bushes. Three of them. There was a massive brute of a Frenchman in a striped jersey, his muscles rippling through the thin material. Next to him was an undersized runt of a man with a sharp, mean face made uglier by the vicious scar that ran its length. To his right lay another civilian, with the thin, keen, controlled face of an ex-regular soldier; his body was turned at the regulation forty-five degree angle, as he fired shot after shot at the trapped patrol.

Schulze raised his machine-pistol, allowing the wet sand to drop from it, and eased off the safety. He gulped in air and, crying, 'All right, frogs. This is it!' pressed the trigger.

Nothing happened!

He pressed it again. Still nothing. He looked down aghast, realizing as the surprised Frenchmen turned round that the wet sand must have jammed the mechanism.

'*Boche!*' Scarface cried in alarm and fired a wild burst. It barely missed Schulze as he rolled to the right. Next moment the big man with the striped jersey raised his rifle and drove the brass butt cruelly into Schulze's side. A heavy boot followed, thudding against his right temple in savage fury. Schulze screamed and blacked out, his head lolling to one side, blood trickling suddenly from the side of his mouth.

Jo-Jo raised his rifle and pointed it directly at the unconscious man's heart. 'I'll finish the Boche pig,' he snarled.

Reynaud knocked away his hand and the rifle exploded harmlessly into the sky. 'My God, Jo-Jo,' he said contemptuously, his keen face flushing suddenly, 'you can't do that to an unconscious men. In cold blood.'

'He's only a Boche,' Jo-Jo grumbled, but he lowered his rifle.

'That's enough, the two of you,' Agnelli ordered. 'All right, come on, we've sown the seed. Let's get the hell out of here before any more of them try the sea trick.'

Hurriedly the three men doubled back the way they had come.

Five minutes later, when the first cautious head peeped round the bushes, the three snipers were already on their way back to Nîmes, leaving the puzzled *Wotan* troopers to attend to a groaning Schulze and wonder what had been the point of the whole business.

THREE

The members of the ambushed patrol were not the only ones who were puzzled by what seemed a purposeless attack. That same evening, The Vulture stared across his desk at Kuno von Dodenburg, while the barracks started to settle down for the night.

'Why?' he kept repeating. 'Why, von Dodenburg? What did they hope to achieve by attacking that patrol? Of course, one man is dead, another seriously wounded, not to mention that rogue Schulze's cracked head – but to what effect?'

Von Dodenburg shrugged. He was just as much in the dark as his CO. 'Frankly, sir, I don't know. Schulze, who fortunately has a lump of cast-iron for a head, tells me that there were three of them – civilians – and the weapons sergeant who examined the empty cartridge cases found on the site of the attack says they are of the type used in non-military rifles, hunting pieces and the like.' He shrugged again, considering. 'So what do we have? A little bunch of amateurs, out to take a potshot at the Boche?'

'Perhaps,' The Vulture agreed. 'Some of those who will never learn that France has been well and truly defeated in the field and do not realize that their politicos under Marshal Petain have come to an arrangement with the *Reich*.' He took off his gold-rimmed monocle, which he affected at times, and polished it deliberately. 'All the same, von Dodenburg, we can't take this lying down. Two attacks on my men in less than ten days! My guess is that we can expect more of the same. They are a decadent people, these southern Frogs. All they think about is their wine and women – and their vices. All the same, there are those among them who have not changed since the days of their fathers and grand-fathers - the *franc-tireurs,* who shot *our* grandfathers and fathers in the back in two wars. Now our problem is this festival in Nîmes which they'll hold in two days' time. As you know the fools at HQ have lifted the curfew regulations. The Frogs will be able to circulate all night without hindrance. Filled up with that disgusting wine of theirs, the hot-heads among them will undoubtedly be out looking for trouble. We must be prepared to nip it in the bud. Agreed?'

'Agreed, sir.'

'Good, from now until this damned festival is over, I want the state of alert of the battalion to be raised from three to one.'

'That's the wartime stage, sir,' von Dodenburg protested. 'The men won't like it. It'll mean no home leave, no local leave. They wont even be allowed to go out of the barracks after darkness. It - '

The Vulture waved him to be silent. 'The men's welfare does not concern me, von Dodenburg. All I am interested in is having the best battalion in the whole of the Army. You and I as regular officers know that one can't have any blot on one's fitness report. Promotion is next to godliness, my old father always used to say.' He grinned momentarily and then frowned, his arrogant face hollowed out to a death's head by the fading light, in which the monocle gleamed like a mirror. 'Heaven, arse and cloudburst, von Dodenburg, what kind of game are those damned Frogs playing behind our backs . . .?'

It was approximately the same thought that General Gilles was expressing to the three attentive Englishmen less than a kilometre away from *Wotan*'s HQ at that very moment, his haughty commanding face wrinkled in bewilderment.

'But to ambush a German patrol,' he was saying, 'on the very stretch of beach we intend to use and so to alert the whole Boche apparatus . . .' he broke off a little helplessly.

'It does seem like a rather nasty coincidence,' The Toff agreed sympathetically, while the other two men eyed the

General's worried face.

'Coincidence? Just now when the Boche are beginning to relax their regulations, some fool goes and takes a potshot at one of their patrols – on *our* beach.'

'Typical ballocks,' Tiddey-Oggy grumbled. He looked a little surprised when the other two laughed. 'What's up?'

'Not very original in yer choice of words, are yer, mate?' Tonsils said with a grin.

'Down in Pompey we don't need the gift of the gab like you smart alecks in the Big Smoke – nor like you airy-fairy public-school blokes with yer cut-glass accents. We're solid folk in Pompey.'

'Yeah,' Tonsils quipped, 'solid – right between the ears.'

'Gentlemen, *please*!' General Gilles commanded, his face revealing total incomprehension of the exchange. 'Back to business.'

Tiddey-Oggy grumbled under his breath but said nothing more. The three Englishmen concentrated their attention on the General.

'Pierre here,' he said, indicating the ex-batman, who squatted at the door, obviously guarding it as if he expected the Germans to break in at any moment, 'has organized the horses for us – and the costumes for us and the girls. Madam has been very helpful there. A good deal of her – er – profits have gone on the black market to pay for them, I'm afraid. The weapons we have from the Germans who were killed at the house, and I have provided myself with a little hardware.' He drew a small pistol fitted with a heavy silencer out of his pocket and grinned a little. 'It is said that generals die in bed, but I can assure you that this particular one will not be taken alive.'

The Toff looked at Tonsils, who nodded; he knew, too, that the General was not bluffing.

Gilles slipped the pistol away and beamed at them. 'One more point, gentlemen. I have heard from my own sources in your country that the submarine is underway. It left two days ago. By now, with a bit of luck it should already be approaching the entrance to the Mediterranean.'

'Hurrah!' the three youths cried spontaneously, their lean

faces lighting up at the thought that help was on its way. At the door, the dour ex-batman frowned, but the General was pleased for them. 'Hurrah indeed, gentlemen.' But we're still a long way from being rescued. There are many dangers, but – *comrades* – ' he emphasized the word with unusual emotion – 'we are prepared. It is my sincerest hope that one week from now, you will be in your own country once again . . .'

Lying back naked on the rumpled, stained bed in the cheap hotel room, half-forgetting the sweat-lathered efforts of the skinny little eighteen-year-old whore to excite his reluctant sexuality, Agnelli told himself that the time had come to betray the General to the Boche. It would be done discreetly, of course. London had insisted on that. There must be no hint of scandal. The blame must lie with the Boche.

The ambush had alerted them, as he had planned it would. Now they were on the look-out for trouble everywhere. He had seen the suspicious looks on the faces of the black-uniformed *SS* pigs outside their barracks, who, obviously suspecting every passer-by, had itchy trigger-fingers. They would shoot first and ask questions afterwards. It would be better if they killed the General than took him alive. That way there would be no need for unnecessary questions.

FOUR

The line of the squall stretched to the horizon, where the heaving mass of the Atlantic met the Spanish coast. Above, a jumbled mass of threatening black clouds and occasional flurries of bitter rain obscured whatever sun there might be.

Slowly and carefully, Lt-Commander Higgs turned the periscope to port so that it made only the smallest possible wave. The mist-shrouded destroyer slid silently into the bright circle of calibrated glass, the sharp outline of her prow softened a little by the water streaming from it.

In the hot, stinking, green-glowing darkness of the submarine, the crew waited tensely for the skipper's identification. There was no sound save that of the bosun whistling *We're gonna hang out our washing on the Siegfried Line* through a gap in his front teeth.

Suddenly Higgs made his identification. 'Enemy destroyer *Moewe* class. Sound battle stations! Right full rudder! All ahead – FULL!'

In a flash, bells clanged all over HMS *Swordfish*. Sailors ran to their battle stations. Operators slipped on their earphones. Higgs wiped his sweating palms on the sides of his trousers, as they all waited in tense expectancy.

'Sound, what bearing?' Higgs asked, when he knew they were all at their stations.

'One propeller, bearing zero-eight-four relative, sir,' the operator answered, with just a suspicion of sudden dryness in his young voice.

Higgs took the periscope up again, his ancient cap turned round, with its peak to the rear. For a moment the heaving waves obscured his vision. 'Up four feet,' he commanded, his voice toneless.

The boat rose. The sharp-prowed silhouette of the German destroyer came into sight again. He could see her white identification number quite clearly on her bow. He sniffed and wondered whether she was out looking for him. He knew he had been strictly commanded not to attack an enemy ship unless he was attacked himself, but the destroyer was a very tempting target to a skipper who had sunk no more than two enemy coastal trawlers on his last trip out in to the North Sea.

'Range?' he demanded.

'Six hundred fifty, sir,' the answer came back in a hurry, as if the crew were well aware of what was going through the skipper's head at this particular moment.

The sonar operator sweated under his headphones as he listened to the frightening *pings* getting ever closer. He turned up the sound so that the Captain could hear. *Ping . . . ping . . . ping . . .*

Higgs could feel the short hairs at the back of his neck stand erect from tension. Instinctively, he realized that the German destroyer had spotted them. They were on a collision course. The victor would be the one who got off the first shots. He made his decision. 'Forward torpedo-room – standing by?'

'Aye, aye, sir,' the torpedo officer's tense voice replied immediately. 'Standing by.'

Hastily Higgs checked the co-ordinates. It would have to be a bow shot. The *pings* grew in intensity until they seemed to fill the whole submarine. The Jerry's sonar must have locked on to them now. Already the sea-drenched seamen would be standing by their deadly depth mines, ready to fire them at the command of the enemy bridge. It was now or never.

'Angle on the bow-port zero-four-three,' the operator called, trying to control his young voice but failing very badly.

'Set!' the bosun growled.

'Down periscope,' Higgs commanded.

The Captain flashed a look around at his men's pale, sickly green faces in the compartment. He knew what they were thinking. His decision might mean sudden death. All the same, excitement tore from man to man, so thick he could almost feel it. It was the excitement of the chase.

'Open outer doors!' Higgs ordered.

'Outer doors opened,' the torpedo officer replied.

'Ready tubes!'

'Tubes ready to fire!'

'Stop,' Higgs commanded, feeling he must shriek with tension, but surprised to hear his voice come out calm and controlled, as if this were a routine training exercise.

'All stop!' The reply echoed through the tense compartment.

'*Ping . . . ping . . . ping . . .*' The noise of approaching enemy craft was almost unbearable.

'FIRE!' Higgs yelled.

The submarine shuddered – once, twice – as the two tons of high-explosive death slid from her tubes.

'Couldn't miss if we tried now, Skipper!' the gunnery officer yelled jubilantly.

'Silence!' Higgs ordered. 'Silence everywhere – at once!' He flung a glance at his wristwatch, timing the duration of the torpedoes' run. Two minutes, he guessed, should do at that range. He followed the green second hand. If the fish didn't explode in two minutes, it meant that they missed their target; then they would really be in trouble.

The submarine rolled slightly. *Once! Twice!*

The crew released their tension in a tremendous cheer. But Higgs had no time for celebrations yet. He wanted to know what had happened on the surface. 'Up periscope,' he commanded urgently.

Hastily, he unfolded the metal handles and watched it slide smoothly up the housing and above the surface of the water. He spun his hat back to front again and pressed his right eye to the sight.

The German destroyer had been hit squarely midships by the two fish. Broken in half, her prow sticking high up in the air, she was sinking fast. Her panic-stricken sailors were diving wildly into the sea from her bow, mouths open in silent screams as they sprang into the burning steam escaping from the fractured boilers. Commander Higgs bit his bottom lip. They were the enemy, all right, but they were also shipwrecked seamen; the unwritten code of the sea demanded that he should do his duty by them.

'We hit her! She's sinking fast.' He silenced the excited cheers of the crew by adding 'There are survivors to be taken aboard. All right, lads, up we go.'

HMS *Swordfish* surfaced in a rain squall. The bitter rain-drops pelted the men on the bridge as the submarine slowly began to edge its way through the debris which bobbed up and down everywhere on the oil-drenched, heaving water.

Higgs ducked his head deeper into his blue duffle-coat, as if he were ashamed of the oil-encrusted lumps of dead flesh which floated face downwards among the debris. He knew it was his duty to kill the King's enemies. All the same he could not laugh at the sight of dead fellow human beings, as some of the men in the tower were doing.

The submarine ploughed on. The pouring rain drowned the steady throb of the diesels, but neither the rain nor the sound of the engines could overpower the screams of the dying and wounded, some of them terribly burnt by the steam, as they bumped against the side of HMS *Swordfish*.

The laughter of the men on the bridge died away.

Higgs tore his eyes away from the lobster-red, naked body of a middle-aged sailor draped over a burning life raft and gave the order to stop.

Without any further command, his men started to pick their way along the slippery, swaying narrow deck of the submarine, grappling hooks in their hands, ready to drag aboard the survivors.

They did not get very far. Suddenly the stern look-out cried out, his young voice full of fear, 'Sir, enemy destroyer closing fast!'

Higgs swung round.

A white bone in her teeth, another destroyer of the *Moewe* class was racing towards the scene at thirty knots, aldis lamp flickering off and on wildly, gunners running towards their turrets.

Higgs did not hesitate. The survivors forgotten now, he screamed, 'Clear the deck! For Christ's sake, move!'

Frantically, the sailors clattered down the tower, sliding the pole into the ship's interior. Higgs followed an instant later, tugging the hatch catches closed and yelling urgently, 'Dive . . . Dive!'

The submarine rocked wildly as the depth charges exploded all around her. Time and time again the lights flickered and threatened to go out. All around the skipper, the crew's faces were ashen and tense with fear, but no one dared to utter even a small cry of shock. Higgs had imposed total silence. Even the engines had been stopped.

Twice the enemy destroyer had passed directly over them, its screw pounding almost earsplittingly through the sonar. Up above, the Germans would be listening for the slightest *ping* from below, and Higgs knew his attempt to convince the Germans that they had sunk him by releasing waste oil and old clothes from the forward torpedo tubes had not worked. They knew he was there and they were out for a kill.

'Prepare stern tubes,' he whispered as the destroyer turned yet once again and prepared for another run over the spot where she knew the British submarine lay.

'Stern tubes loading, sir . . . Opening outer doors now. Open, Skipper.'

Higgs waited momentarily.

'Ready all tubes, sir!' The report he had been waiting for came through in a horse whisper, as the *ping . . . ping* of the approaching destroyer came ever closer. It was now or never.

'*Fire one – fire two!*' he yelled.

At the stern the gunnery officer slammed down the firing keys. There was a faint hiss of compressed air. Once more the submarine shuddered, as the deadly fish slid out of their tubes to commence their deadly run.

The first torpedo struck home, sending a metallic *crump* reverberating through the submarine's hull. One instant later the second torpedo smashed into the destroyer.

'Up periscope!' Higgs commanded.

The tube hissed upwards. The impact of the explosion had forced the German destroyer to heel over, exposing her red-painted hull. Flames and thick, black, oily smoke were shooting high into the grey wet sky. Blazing chunks of wreckage were showering the sea, sending up spouts of white water.

'We got her!' he announced with no elation in his voice, although he had done what no British sub skipper had done so far in this war – he had sunk two enemy destroyers in one day. He knew the survivors would report the presence of a British submarine heading for the entrance to the Mediterranean. Now the Jerries knew they were coming. In spite of the excited laughter and cries all around him, he knew with the certainty of a vision that HMS *Swordfish* would never come back from this journey. He looked around at the crew's happy eager faces and told himself that they had only a matter of days to live.

FIVE

Fireworks shot into the burning afternoon sky and exploded to shower the cheering, happy, drunken crowd staring up at the display with red and white stars. Bands played – *java* and the *sardana* of Catalonia – and the townspeople danced in the cobbled streets. Proudly, swarthy men in their tight, best black clothes rode around the arena in which the bulls were already being perpared for the evening's sport, and flashing-eyed women in long floral dresses rode side-saddle behind them, flirting outrageously above their fans. The annual Nîmes festival had begun.

But on this day another kind of entertainment was going to be provided for the citizens of Nîmes, of a kind unknown to the port since the days fifteen centuries before when the Germanic hordes, half-naked barbarians in bearskins, had descended upon the Roman city, looting and pillaging.

'*Make way for Wotan! . . . The street free for the SS . . . Clear the road there! . . . Hurry, hurry . . . The SS marches!*' Sergeant-Major Metzger's angry voice echoed frighteningly down the narrow streets.

Nine abreast, the brass band of *SS Assault Battalion Wotan* swung round the corner of the road which led to the Roman arena, the centre of the festival. Musical instruments glittered blindingly in the sun. At its head came the massive drum major, bigger even than The Butcher and resplendent in his immaculate black uniform with white and red epaulettes. He swung his mace with majestic ease, his gaze fixed on some distant horizon remote from the inferior, decadent French world all around him.

Marching at the head of his company and just behind the

125

standard bearer, carrying the hooked black cross of the battalion with its bloody motto DEATH OR DISHONOUR, Captain von Dodenburg, clad in black leather with the proud black and white Knight's Cross bouncing at his throat, cried above the silver clash of the band, 'A song!'

Behind him, Metzger, still heavily bandaged, bellowed, 'A song, one, two three!'

Two hundred strong, harsh voices burst into the proud song of the summer of 1940, overpowering the band.

'*Denn, wir fahren . . . denn wir fahren . . . gegen Eng-ge-land**

'*Kommt die Kunde ich bin gefallen . . .*

'*Denn wir fahren gegen England . . .*'

Striding out at the head of his company von Dodenburg felt himself overcome by a burning sense of pride. His young men were worthy representatives of the New Germany, cleansed of the decadence, corruption and sloth of the old continent. He could see both fear and envy in the eyes of the abruptly silent civilians who lined both sides of the street. He knew that they knew they were in the presence of the representatives of a new age: the arrogant symbol of German power – of the German Century.

It had been The Vulture's idea. 'A show of strength,' he had called it, so that the 'natives' would learn to respect German strength and power. The sight of one of *Wotan*'s élite companies in full marching order would ensure peace right from the start of the festival. Now Captain von Dodenburg, who had been doubtful at the outset, knew The Vulture had been correct. The natives were indeed impressed.

Up in the attic, crouched over his telescopic rifle, ex-Captain Reynaud tensed as the hard stamp of boots on cobbles, the tingle of the brass and the sound of the harsh, arrogant voices grew ever closer.

He was excited yet calm. In the hamlet where his battalion had so nearly won its last battle against the hated Boche, he

* Roughly, 'We are going to ride against England.'

had wanted to die a hero's death in combat, or that of a martyr at the hands of German firing squad for having shot the captured *SS* officer. But abruptly, during that breakdown and the flight of what was left of the battalion, his courage had vanished. He, too, had run with the rest of the rabble. Ashamed, throughout the week afterwards he had drunk himself into insensibility. Then Agnelli had found him and forced him to pull himself together. The little ambush on the beach had restored his courage and self-esteem. Today, before the eyes of the whole of Nîmes, he would show the Boche and his fellow Frenchmen that not all of the *grande nation* were prepared to submit to Boche tyranny. He tucked the rifle butt more firmly into his shoulder, his dark eyes gleaming with pride and hatred, and waited.

Proudly swinging his silver mace before his massive chest, the drum major bore round the corner, leading the band. Ahead the ancient arena loomed, boxed in on both sides by shabby, tall, eighteenth-century houses, from which bright garlands hung and from whose windows civilians gaped, wide-eyed and awed by the tremendous power of the marching men.

Captain von Dodenburg bellowed, 'First Company *Assault Battalion Wotan – parade march!*' Without the slightest hesitation, the giants, burdened by their thirty-kilo packs, rifles and heavy steel helmets, broke into the goose step, bringing up their legs as high as their waist, then slapping the steel-shot boots down on the cobbles again. The narrow stone alley reverberated with the fearsome noise.

The sight of that march being carried out in the heart of his homeland was too much for Reynaud. He swung his rifle round until the handsome, sweating face of the leather-clad captain swept into the calibrated glass. For one brief instant, Reynaud thought he had seen it somewhere before, then he squeezed the trigger.

Below, the standard bearer screamed shrilly. With his free hand he clutched his chest and watched in horror as his own blood started to stain the hooked cross a bright scarlet. Slowly his knees began to buckle beneath him. He dropped the banner, falling forward on to the cobbles. For one long moment there was absolute silence. The entire column had come to a halt. Captain von Dodenburg at its head stood gazing down at the dead man lying sprawled over the bloody banner, who he knew had taken the bullet meant for him.

Then all hell was let loose. Women screamed. Gendarmes blew their whistles shrilly. German NCOs and officers bellowed orders. Everywhere the *SS* troopers broke ranks, pushing into the crowd, unslinging their rifles while they searched for the unknown sniper. Reynaud fired again. An *SS* man clapped his wounded shoulder and dropped his rifle with a curse. The crowd panicked, fighting and shoving each other frantically to get out of the line of fire. Others flung themselves on the ground, hands over their ears or heads as if that would protect them. 'Look out, the swine will fire again!' they yelled in terror, pushing the *SS* troopers forward to protect them.

Captain von Dodenburg, pistol in hand, searched the right side of the road, eyes sweeping the now empty balconies. Matz and Schulze covered his back with their rifles. He knew he was a perfect target and knew, too, that the sniper was out to get him, but he must find the man. It was a matter of prestige. If the sniper managed to get away, the news would be all over France the following day that *a lone Frenchman had managed to panic an entire Boche SS company!* No, Germany could not afford that kind of publicity, and he dared not even think what The Vulture's reaction would be if he reported the sniper had got away.

There was another sharp crack. The slug missed him by millimetres. He ducked instinctively, feeling the stone splinters from the wall which it struck splatter his face.

'*Vive General Gilles! . . . Vive la resistance! . . . Vive la France!*' . . . the hoarse, excited voice cried down at the cowering crowd of civilians.

Then von Dodenburg spotted him, hanging out of an attic window of the third house to his right. 'Surround that building!' he bellowed. 'Front and back! At the double!'

The Germans pelted towards the house, stamping cruelly over the civilians who lay everywhere. The sniper fired again. A soldier stopped, as if he had just run into a brick wall.

Von Dodenburg swung round on Matz and Schulze. 'You two, follow me!'

Crouched low, they ran towards the house, as slugs whistled around them. As they clattered up the rickety stairs that smelled of cat urine, stale food and ancient lecheries, a toothless crone with a beard, her skinny body trembling violently, tried to bar their way, clinging to von Dodenburg like a long-lost son in her fear. Brutally, he shoved her to one side and continued his progress.

When they reached the landing. Von Dodenburg looked at the several doors in breathless bewilderment. Behind which was the sniper? Then the acrid smell of cordite assailed his nostrils and he knew the man they sought was in the middle room. 'Schulze,' he commanded, 'cover that door!'

'Am I to go in, sir?' Matz rapped, no trace of fear in his voice.

'No, you are to come with me. Come on!'

Together they raced to the end of the landing.

'Bend!' von Dodenburg ordered, thrusting his pistol back in its holster. He sprang on to Matz's back. With his helmeted head he rammed open the trap door that led on to the roof and heaved himself up.

'What are you going to do, sir?' Matz asked in alarm.

'Tackle him from where he won't expect us – the balcony to the front.'

'But, sir,' Matz protested, 'that's suicide. Let me and Schulze go in through the door!'

'No, I'm not risking any more of my men's lives. I'm doing it this way. You stand by here and help Schulze. Clear?'

'Clear, sir,' Matz said miserably.

A moment later Captain von Dodenburg disappeared on to the steep, tiled roof.

Reynaud paused for a moment and wiped the sweat from

his dark face with a hand that trembled slightly. He was scared. but not overly frightened. He knew they had him surrounded. It was what he had expected. He and Agnelli had discussed the sacrifice he would be forced to make. Just as he had been leaving on that day, the little, scar-faced resistance man had shaken his hand and had said solemnly, 'Paul, don't let them take you alive. Remember the sacrifice you will have to make will be for France. It will live on for ever, an inspiration to our whole nation. You understand?'

'I understand,' he had answered with equal solemnity. Now that the time had come he was not afraid. Carefully, he started to fit his last magazine. The last bullet would be for himself, but he would take five Boche with him. He lifted the rifle and fired once more.

Carefully, Captain von Dodenburg started to edge his way along the slate roof which sloped down at almost fifty degrees. It was no easy task but, he told himself, it was the only way. One slip and he would be over the side, falling fifty metres to the cobbles below.

He inched his way across ten metres. then fifteen, twenty. In a moment he would be in position at the edge of the guttering; there he intended to drop on to the sniper's balcony, some five metres below. Biting his bottom lip, he started on the last stretch, an area of slate covered with the slippery green moss.

Suddenly, he was sliding feet first, fingers scrabbling for a hold! Below, there was a gasp of horror from his men. His feet went over the lead guttering. The ground loomed up frighteningly. *He was going over!* A cry of fear died on his lips as his fingers sought and found a hold. Pain shot through his right arm as the guttering ripped off all the nails of his right hand. Still he held on: it was his only hope.

Forcing himself to keep calm, he reached up and caught the gutter with his left hand taking the strain off his right shoulder which seemed about to pull the arm out of its socket. For a moment he hung there gratefully, breathing shallowly.

He knew he could not hang there long. Somehow he had to haul himself up again. Flexing his muscles, he started to heave, blood pouring down his arm from his savaged fingers.

Miraculously, he made it and lay face down on the guttering, his heart pounding like a sledge hammer.

By sheer effort of will, he forced himself to his knees, trying to forget the terrible trembling which racked his body. Taking a deep breath, he started to crawl along the guttering, holding on to the steel fire-hooks in case the brittle lead piping gave way under him. Finally he reached the part of the roof overlooking the balcony. From that angle it seemed very small: a shabby little square of concrete lined with flower pots and enclosed by a rickety iron railing. He would have to drop with his back to the road below so that when – *if*, a cynical little voice at the back of his mind said – he reached the balcony, he could go straight in at the sniper and catch him off guard.

Captain von Dodenburg stared hard at the small square of concrete and the cobbles far below, fighting the wave of fear and nausea which threatened to overcome him. He drew a deep breath, took his pistol out and placed it on the guttering in front of him. Gingerly, he turned around and thrust his legs over the edge of the roof. Holding on with one hand, he thrust the pistol into his belt. With a hasty prayer, he lowered himself over the side. For one long moment he hung in mid-air, his body swaying wildly as he prepared for the jump. 'NOW!' he commanded himself and launched himself into space.

He hit the balcony with a crash. His legs seemed to thrust deep into his stomach, causing him to feel sick. But there was no time for that. The man with the rifle had seen him and was raising his weapon. Von Dodenburg did not have time to draw his pistol. He dove headfirst through the window and crashed directly into the sniper. They fell together in a wild heap, cursing and snarling at each other as they twisted back and forth on the cartridge-littered floor trying to find an advantage.

Suddenly von Dodenburg's bloody fingers found a hold – the Frenchman's nostrils. He did not hesitate but thrust two fingers inside his nose – and yanked hard. The Frenchman screamed as the membrane was ripped apart. In his agony, he released his hold. Von Dodenburg crooked his arm, then with all his force he slammed his elbow into the sniper's jaw. The man's head clicked back with a fearful snap. Next moment his body went limp, and an exhausted von Dodenburg collapsed on top of the unconscious Frenchman like a spent lover.

SIX

'Well?' The Vulture demanded.

'Nothing, sir,' von Dodenburg answered, a blood-stained handkerchief wrapped around his hand which throbbed agonizingly.

'You mean he refuses to speak, the Frog swine, after he has killed two of my men and wounded five more?' He slapped his riding crop across his desk angrily, as if it were a personal insult.

'I'm afraid so, sir.'

'Well, I'm not going to have it. The swine must speak. I want to know whether this has anything to do with this damned General Gilles we have been ordered to look for.'

'He did shout the name into the street and he is an ex-soldier.' Swiftly, von Dodenburg explained how the prisoner had once ordered him shot when he had been captured at the fight for the mountain barrier.

The Vulture pondered the information, then said. 'All right, von Dodenburg, go and have that hand of yours dressed. I'll handle this matter myself.'

Captain von Dodenburg hesitated momentarily. There was an unholy look in The Vulture's ice-blue eyes. Then he shrugged. The prisoner's fate was sealed anyway. He had shot a German soldier. The punishment was death. He saluted and went out.

The Vulture waited a moment, then pressed the bell on his desk.

The Butcher came in, as if he had been listening at the door. 'Wheel in the Frog prisoner, sir?' he asked eagerly.

The Vulture looked at him coldly. 'One day, Sergeant-

Major, you're going to get a nasty pain in the ear from listening at keyholes,' he snapped. 'Yes, wheel him in.'

Five minutes later, The Butcher pushed Reynaud through the door with a harsh, 'In there, Frog, before I kick yer Frog-ass in.'

The Frenchman only prevented himself from falling by grabbing The Vulture's desk.

The Vulture reacted by slashing his cane over the man's fingers, sending him reeling, 'Don't you dare touch my desk, you treacherous pig!' he snorted.

Reynaud swayed dangerously in front of the German officer, gaps where his front teeth had been, the blood caked black under his broken nose. 'I am a French officer,' he said thickly. 'I demand to be treated as a prisoner of war.'

'So you speak German, do you? Then let me tell you something. You are not a French officer. You are not a civilian. You are nothing, for you are already *dead*!' He allowed the dark-faced Frenchman time to absorb the information and then said, 'You have killed German soldiers and will be killed accordingly. The only right you still have, Frenchman, is to decide how you will spend the next few hours.'

'What?'

'I think you understood, Frenchman.' The Vulture pointed his cane at Reynaud. 'Do you want to scream for death – or do you want to make your last hours on this earth as pleasant as they can be under the circumstances?'

'What do you want from me?' Reynaud asked.

The Vulture could see that he was afraid by the fluttering of his prominent Adam's apple.

'I want information and I want it fast.'

Reynaud shook his head, his lips compressed tightly together.

The Vulture shrugged carelessly. 'Have it your way, Frenchman.' He jerked his head at a waiting Metzger. 'Strip him,' he commanded.

The Butcher reached out a mighty paw to seize the Frenchman's blood-stained shirt and grunted. The shirt came away in his hand, revealing weals on his skinny body where the cell guards had already taken their revenge for the death of their comrades. Another grunt and the man's shabby trousers and underpants followed.

The Vulture nodded his approval. He knew a naked man always feels inferior and defenceless in the presence of those who are fully-clothed. 'I am going to ask you what you know of a certain General Gilles – you shouted his name to the crowd, didn't you – and where he is now?'

Reynaud held his head proudly, but he could already feel his knees beginning to tremble at the thought of what must come.

'All right, Metzger, rape him,' he ordered in a bored voice.

Metzger needed no urging. His big steel-shot boot lashed out and caught the prisoner directly between his skinny buttocks, sending him flying against the wall, where he sank to the ground moaning pitifully.

The Vulture rose to his feet deliberately and looked down at the heap of white naked flesh contemptuously. 'Stand up, dog! You're going to be sitting for the rest of your miserable life once we have broken your legs.' He reached down and, grabbing Reynaud's mop of hair, dragged him to his feet. 'Are you going to make it easy for yourself now?'

Reynaud, his eyes full of tears of pain, shook his head.

The Vulture's knee rose sharply, feigning a kick in the groin. Reynaud doubled instinctively. The Vulture's fist lashed out, sending him flying across the room towards Metzger. The Butcher struck him another blow with his boot, ripping the flesh off his buttocks with the steel studs, and sent Reynaud flying back to The Vulture once more.

For five terrible minutes while the two Germans played their little game, the only sounds to be heard were the anguished cries of pain from their victim and their own heavy breathing.

Finally, The Vulture said, 'Enough – for the moment, Metzger. I think we've carried out the initial softening-up correctly.'

135

Gratefully, only half-conscious, the naked Frenchman sank to the floor, his body covered with ugly red bruises, blood oozing out of his broken nose once more.

The Vulture looked down at him contemptuously. 'So, my French friend, you want to take a little rest, eh?'

Reynaud did not respond.

'Soon you'll be resting for ever,' The Vulture continued insidiously. 'But if you sing, you can stay there in peace until the execution command comes. Now then where is General Gilles?'

Weakly the prisoner shook his battered head. 'I . . . don't know,' he whispered.

'Oh, but yes you do, Frenchman,' The Vulture snapped, his narrow face flushing angrily again. He turned to a waiting Metzger. 'Give me your dirk,' he ordered.

The Butcher whipped out his NCO's dirk and handed it to his CO wordlessly.

'Put the Frog on that stool there.'

The Butcher lifted up the naked man as if he were a child and plonked him down heavily on the Army issue three-legged stool with a slit in the middle. When Reynaud sagged The Butcher grabbed him cruelly by the hair and yanked his head. 'Get that damned Frog turnip of yours up,' he snarled, 'and look at the CO.'

Reynaud looked at the German's wavering, blurred outline through eyes that were already puffed up and almost closed.

Casually, biding his time, The Vulture felt the blade of the dirk with his forefinger and thumb. 'Sharp, very sharp,' he whispered, almost as if he were talking to himself. 'You must be congratulated, Sergeant-Major, on the way you keep your side-arm in perfect condition.'

'Thank you, sir,' Metzger said happily.

There was a long silence. The Vulture continued to run his finger along the sharp little blade while Reynaud watched him with horrified eyes.

'They tell me,' The Vulture broke the silence at last, 'that you Frenchmen place great store by physical love.

You all fancy yourselves as – er – great swordsmen.' He smiled menacingly and The Butcher guffawed. 'A Frenchman without his nuts would not be very highly regarded, I have heard.'

'What are you going to do?' Reynaud gasped.

'Play a little game with you, Frenchman. That's all, an exciting little game.' He looked down at Reynaud's genitals significantly, and the prisoner trembled violently, anticipating what was to come.

The Vulture did not take his eyes off the prisoner when he commanded Metzger to commence; they fixed him with almost hypnotic intensity. Then when he saw that the Sergeant-Major was ready, he bent down and thrust the dirk under the stool so that its razor-sharp point was positioned just below a terrified Reynaud's genitals. 'NOW!' he snapped.

Metzger raised Reynaud by the hair, slapped his face with his free hand so that his head swung from side to side and let him drop again almost in the same instant. Reynaud screamed with pain as the dirk slashed into his body. He shot up again, only to be caught by Metzger and slapped once more.

Twice Reynaud fainted from the pain and twice Metzger revived him with a bucket of cold water. By now his genitals were a bloody mess, nicked and slashed everywhere by the dirk's sharp point.

The Vulture stared down at his limp and bloodied body. 'I repeat my question. Where is General Gilles? And I must tell you now that I have finished playing with you. Next time I am going to get very serious. Well?'

Stubbornly Reynaud shook his head, not trusting himself to speak any more.

The Vulture thrust the dirk directly through the hole so that perhaps half its length protruded above the seat. 'You realize what will happen if you fall on that more than once. Metzger, pick him up.'

The Butcher gathered up the trembling Frenchman in his massive arms and waited with the prisoner poised directly above the stool.

The Vulture tightened his hold on the dirk. 'I shall count up to three and then I shall order the Sergeant-Major to drop you. *One . . . two . . .*' He hesitated for a mere fraction of a second, his lips parted already for the first syllable of the final word.

Reynaud could take no more. In hysterical gasps, he began to tell them about Agnelli and how he had volunteered for the suicide mission to raise the flag of the resistance in Provence.

'Give him a glass of water,' The Vulture ordered when the Frenchman paused for breath.

He waited until Reynaud had drunk it greedily, through broken lips which were caked with black blood. 'Now,' he said, 'where is this damned General Gilles of yours hiding?'

'I don't know – it is the truth, I do not,' Reynaud said pleadingly. 'I served under him in the war. After the last battle, he disappeared.' He looked from one to another of the hard German faces desperately. 'He *disappeared*. There was a rumour that his ex-batman was hiding him somewhere in Provence –'

'You know that he is going to try to escape by sea, don't you?' The Vulture cut him short brutally. 'Now out with it, man!' He raised the blood-stained dirk again. 'Where and when?'

'I don't – ' the words died in Reynaud's throat.

The Vulture leaned forward and turned the point of the dirk in the bloody mess between his legs.

'*I'll tell you!*' he screamed. '*I'll tell you! But no more, please, please.*' He held up his hands in supplication.

The Vulture was completely unmoved. 'Where and when?'

'I don't know the hour, but some time during the *concours de manades* tomorrow they are going to attempt to leave the town, Agnelli told me. It is the truth.'

The Vulture smiled at Metzger in triumph. The *concours de menades* was the game of skill the locals played with the bulls. Instead of killing them like the Spaniards did, bold local youths would attempt to seize a cockade fixed between the bull's horns. 'And where?'

'Again, I don't know – ' The Vulture held up his dirk

threateningly, and Reynaud hurriedly added, 'But some-where on the beach to the south of Nîmes.'

The Vulture dropped the blood-stained dirk on to his desk with an air of finality. 'Take him out, Sergeant-Major, and have him shot. See the firing squad aim true and finish him the first time. He *was* a brave man . . .

Five: Escape from Nîmes

'Now let me say this. The CO swears he'll have the eggs off any section commander who lets the Frenchman escape, *with a blunt razor-blade!*'

Capt von Dodenburg, July 1940

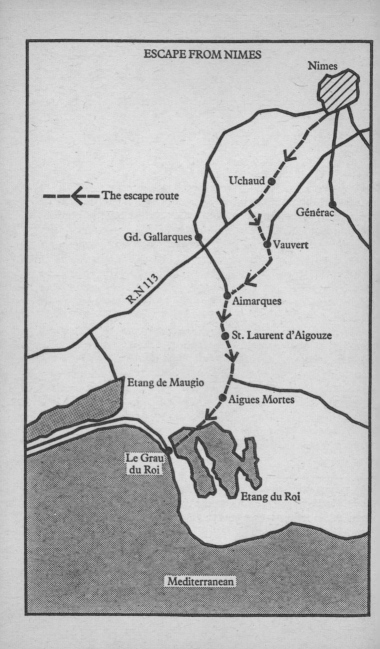

ONE

Slowly and carefully, like a timid whale, HMS *Swordfish* surfaced. As the water ran off her deck, the bright moonlight bathed the conning tower and gave it a shimmering, wraith-like appearance. With her diesels thudding away softly, the long ghostly shape slid into the bay, while Lt-Commander Higgs surveyed the coastline with his night glasses. The men on the bridge with him were excited now that they had finally reached the rendezvous, but there was something about the vast hush of the night that made them keep silent and hold their peace.

Then Higgs found what he sought: the characteristic outline of the coast off Le Grau du Roi and, behind it, shimmering silver in the moonlight, the lake – Etang du Roi. He lowered his glasses, satisfied, and announced, 'We're right on target. We've reached our destination. But it's going to be difficult if we have a full moon tonight like this,' he mused aloud, unconsciously communicating his own private fears to the others.

'Anyone who's lived in a tin cigar like this for any length of time, Skipper, is already living with one foot in the grave,' the bosun, standing behind him, said stoutly. 'I've been in the submarine service since 'thirty-six, when I transferred from battle-wagons, and I told myself right from the start – even in peacetime – that you've got to live with the possibility you ain't coming back.'

'Proper ray of sunshine you are, Chief,' a rating commented sourly. 'You'll have me crying me bleeding eyes out in half a mo.'

'And you'll be getting a knuckle sandwich in half a mo,

if you don't watch that lip of yours, Jones,' the bosun growled, flexing his muscles so that the fading dancing girl engraved on his shoulder did a quick shimmy.

'All right, all right, you two,' Higgs said with a grin. 'Save your energy for the Jerries. You might just need it.'

'*Grr.*' The bosun bared his big teeth. 'I eat Jerries for breakfast.'

'Take her down,' Higgs said. 'You lot are getting too much fresh air. It's going to your heads. Back to the fug.'

A minute later, the submarine had disappeared beneath the gleaming cold, still surface of the Mediterranean as quietly as she had emerged.

It was two o'clock on the morning of the second day of the festival . . .

It was still dark outside, though already the horizon was beginning to be tinged that light purple which is characteristic of summer dawn in the south. But all was purposeful activity in the barracks of *SS Assault Battalion Wotan.* From the cookhouse there came the rattle of dixies and the smell of boiling coffee. At the tank sheds, the mechanics and drivers were warming up their engines, and there were lights everywhere in the barrack rooms and offices.

Von Dodenburg had assembled his company to brief them in the chapel. Against a background of candles and gaudy holy pictures above the flamboyant altar, with the air heavy with the scent of incense, he told his keen-eyed, attentive troopers what their mission was going to be this day.

'We move out at five hundred hours. Our task is to look for a French general named Gilles – a description and photograph of him will be handed out to each platoon and section commander – who the CO believes will attempt to make for the coast today. The General is expecting to be picked up there by a British vessel. The Navy has already been alerted to handle that end of the business. We have definite information that the French general will use the cover of the local festival to make his escape.'

For a moment the vision of the dead Frenchman, shouting a defiant *Vive la France* and waving the blindfold away scornfully before they had shot him on the range last night, flashed through his brain, and he wondered how The Vulture had got the information out of such a brave man. Then he dismissed the thought quickly; it was not wise to ponder such things.

'Our mission is to block the *Route National* 113 and all the minor roads leading off it to the sea. That is a large assignment. We are going to be thin on the ground, but there is no tother way to tackle it. We'll break down into sections and set up road blocks here, here, here and here.' He pointed out the sites on the big map propped against a gaudy statue of the Virgin Mary. 'Now let me say this. The CO swears – to use his own classic phrase – he'll have the eggs off any section commander who lets the Frenchman escape, *with a blunt razor-blade!*'

The men laughed uneasily.

'And for any section that apprehends him, there will be tin all round. The Black Heinrich* First Class for the section commander and the Third for his men. *Plus* seven days' leave in Paris!'

There was a hum of excited talk, and Schulze whispered to Matz, 'Hold me, Matzi, I think I'm going to faint! *Brother!*'

'Get off it,' Matz snarled in his usual early morning black mood. 'Everybody knows you don't like girls.'

Around them the young troopers laughed at the exchange, and Von Dodenburg held up his hands for silence. 'All right,' he said, 'that's about it. But remember this. It is vital for the peace which now exists between the *Reich* and France that this Frenchman does not escape. For if he does, he will be the rallying point for many Frenchmen who wish to continue the war. Gilles is no better than a war-monger, and I think all of us, veteran and new recruit,

* Army slang for the Iron Cross.

145

have had enough of war.' He smiled at them. 'Let's play soldiers for the time being. All right, off you go and get your nigger-sweat.'

Hastily the men marched out towards the cookhouse where the nigger-sweat – acorn coffee – was already waiting for them.

It was four o'clock.

'Sweet Jesus!' Tiddey-Oggy grumbled as he put the final touches to his immaculate white outfit, consisting of shirt, trousers and shoes, with a red sash around the waist the only touch of colour.' I feel like one of them nancy boys yer see parading up and down Shaftesbury Avenue in London.'

'Yeah,' Tonsils agreed happily, putting on his lacquered black sombrero. 'Every time you bend down in them trousers, I get excited.'

'Ballocks!'

'What a charming gift with words you have,' Tonsils quipped.

'More ballocks.'

'*She'll be wearing khaki knickers when she comes, Oh, she'll be wearing khaki knickers when she comes . . .*' The Toff was singing happily to the tune of *She'll be coming round the Mountains* as he dressed in his costume, which, according to the General, would identify him as a cowboy from the near-by Camargue. 'How do I look, chaps?' he asked, pirouetting in his baggy trousers, white silken shirt and flat black hat.

'Like the sodding fairy prince. Tight as a drum, never been done,' Tiddey-Oggy growled, pulling on his skin-tight boots.

Tonsils blew him a kiss. 'Lov-erly,' he breathed.

The Toff grinned happily. 'I say, chaps, try to be a little serious. Do you think I'll pass as Pancho from the Pampas?'

'Of course,' a voice from the door said. 'Your costumes are excellent.'

It was the General, dressed in the white costume of a *razeteur*, whose role in the running of the bulls was to seize

146

the cockade from between the bull's horns. 'I feel a little long in the tooth for this sort of thing, but I'm sure that the Boche won't realize that.'

'If I may say so, sir,' The Toff said, 'you look quite spot on.'

The General beamed, although he did not fully understand the English expression. 'Now then, this is the order of march. Madame and her – er – ladies will precede us, joining the *abrivado* as it passes the house.'

'*Abrivado?*' Tiddey-Oggy queried. 'What's that when it's at home?'

'It is a dialect word. It means the arrival of the bulls in the town. They'll be driven in by the men of Camargue – ' He nodded at The Toff – 'the local cowboys and their girl-friends. We *razeteurs* and *tourneurs*, our assistants* – ' he indicated the other two Guardsmen – 'will follow. Clear?'

'Clear,' they said in unison.

'Once the festivities are underway and the crowd is excited, one group of cowboys, *razeteurs* and *tourneurs*, plus their bulls, will stage a private *bandido*.' He raised his hand just as Tiddey-Oggy opened his mouth to speak. 'Again a local dialect word,' he explained. 'It means the same thing as the *abrivado* only in reverse. We drive the bulls out of the town back to the pasture, performing our deadly little art as we do so.'

'But hang on, General,' Tonsils said hastily, his face suddenly pale. 'Mrs Mortimore's handsome son is a town boy from the Big Smoke. He doesn't know nothing about herding bulls. Those sods look mighty dangerous to me.'

'Ah, but my dear fellow, you are forgetting Madame,' the General said easily.

'*Madame!*'

'Yes, Madame. You must know that before she took up her – um – vocation, she was a simple country girl from the Camargue. She knows a lot about bulls and horses.'

'Aye,' Tiddey-Oggy added grimly, 'and she's had plenty of experience herding cows ever since. But carry on, General.'

* The *razeteur*'s assistant, whose job it is to excite the bull.

147

'Thank you.' The General bowed ironically. 'Madame will be in charge of the steers. But please, gentlemen, look for yourself. She must be mounted up by now.'

Curiously, the three Englishmen crowded around the attic window and peered down, where, surrounded by her girls, who were clad in the flamboyant full-length dress of the area and sported red roses behind their right ears in the Provençal fashion, Madame waited.

She was dressed completely in black, save for a white blouse, and was mounted on a patient horse which sagged dangerously in the middle under her weight. Clenched in her teeth was a flower! She must have become aware that they were staring down at her, for she looked up suddenly like some great, overblown fertility goddess and then gracefully tossed the flower up at them.

'Oh, my sainted aunt!' The Toff breathed in awe and ducked just as the horse took its first hesitant steps, air streaming out of its nostrils with the strain like small grey clouds.

It was now dawn.

The peasants were streaming in from all directions. Old men in rusty black smocks, their faces the colour of saddle-leather, swigged the fierce local red wine from bottles as they marched. Behind them, dressed in their annual finery, their womenfolk tottered on unaccustomed high heels. Children were everywhere, clad in their Sunday best, squealing and running with excitement. At regular intervals among the crowds came the bands, their pipes shrilling, the kettle-drums rattling, setting the children off dancing in crazy circles, which did not even break when they reached the road block guarded by the grim-faced, blond giants with the gleaming silver runes of the *SS* on their collars.

Schulze pushed back his helmet from his sweaty brow and said to one group of dancing children, 'Piss off, kids! Can't you see we want to play soldier?' But he smiled as he spoke.

'You like kids?' Matz enquired lazily.

'Yer, when they're blond and eighteen and have tits sticking up so much yer scared yer get yer eyes poked out.

Ner, I don't mind 'em. Funny lot, the Frogs, ain't they?'

'What do you mean, Schulze?' Matz asked, taking his eyes off a black-haired beauty riding side-saddle, whose skirt had ridden up to reveal that she had forgotten to put on a very essential part of her underwear.

'Well, they didn't exactly put up much of a show in the campaign. They had their legs under their arms most of the time, making dust.'

'Rather ferk than fight, you mean?'

'Sort of. But look at that lot of silly sods.' He indicated a group of excited, black-haired youths, clad in blinding white. 'You know what they're going to be doing soon?'

'No, Schulze.'

''ell, I'll tell you, bird-brain, because you ain't cultured like me. It's an old custom. The silly sods are gonna grab coloured balls off the horns of bulls. Fancy that, Matzi.'

'I don't, mate, thank you very kindly.'

'Well, what I'm saying is this. It takes a lot of courage to do that kind of thing, so why did they bugger off on the battlefield?'

Before Matz had a chance to answer the question, a single rocket hissed into the blue sky and burst into a ball of grey smoke above the *arenes de Nîmes*, the signal to start the second day of the festival. It was greeted by a great roar from the throng streaming towards the centre and followed a moment later by clapping of hands.

Matz rubbed the sweat off his brow with his sleeve, feeling the sun, already climbing higher into the intense blue of the July sky, beginning to burn on his back uncomfortably. 'It's gonna be a scorcher today, Schulze,' he said.

'You're sodding right there,' Schulze agreed.

It was six o'clock on the morning of 11 July 1940. Unknown to those who were to play a role on this day, the direction of France's future would be decided in this remote, hot, provincial town.

TWO

The festival exploded with gaiety. The cobbled streets of the centre of the old town were packed solid with its drunken, singing, red-faced, happy citizens; they kept behind the wooden barriers of the *course de rues* only with difficulty, passing five-litre leather bottles to each other and laughing outrageously when someone missed finding his mouth and squirted his face crimson with the wine.

'Here they come!' someone cried.

'Here they come!' The cry was taken up everywhere. All eyes shot to the left as the first of the bulls skidded round the corner and halted suspiciously as it saw the packed masses. It stood in the sun, the great hump of muscle on its neck swollen tight and steam coming from its nostrils in hard pointed streams, as it pawed the cobbles with its right hoof.

Suddenly the bull charged. A boy in white waved a yellow cape in front of it. The animal changed direction, puzzled, and slammed into a wooden barrier, sending it trembling along its whole length and forcing the spectators to retreat in delight and fear.

This was the opportunity the *razeteur* had been awaiting. As the bull backed off, pulling out its horns with an audible thwack, he darted forward and grabbed for the cockade which was attached to the animal's right horn with elastic.

'He's got it!' the crowd cried ecstatically.

But the elastic would not break. The boy tugged again. Too late. The bull swung round, its red eyes glaring and with half a ton of solid muscle behind it, it ran its leather-covered horns into the youth. He went down, pole-axed under the bull's flying hooves, and lay still there, while half a dozen *tourneurs* sprang over the barriers, waving their capes wildly in order to attract the bull's attention before it started to gore the unconscious youth.

While the puzzled bull dashed back and forth, civilians raced into the arena and dragged the boy away.

'Great heaven,' The Toff breathed in Tonsils' ear, 'and they call this a game!'

'You can say that again, mate,' Tonsils whispered, awed.

The General smiled at them. 'It is a matter of proving their manliness,' he explained.

'I'd sooner do it in bed any day,' Tonsils answered.

'Wait till you see the professionals in the *course royale* when they take the protective covering off the bull's horns. Then you can really expect the blood to flow.'

'I can do without that,' The Toff answered.

'Don't worry.' The General flashed a look at his wristwatch, saying, 'As soon as the *course royale* starts to warm up we're going to stage our own little private show. *Ne c'est pas, Madame?*' he added in French, looking up at Madame on her horse.

She flashed him a gold-toothed smile, her bosom trembling like jelly as the horse attempted to shift her weight a little by stamping its right foreleg. 'Naughty boy, General,' she said, wagging a finger at him. 'You're not trying to play games with a defenceless little girl, are you?'

The General bowed gallantly. 'Of course not, Madame! I wouldn't dare. I was just telling my young English comrades here that our own little game will commence soon.'

'*La, la,*' she minced. 'I know the little games you men always want to play with defenceless women.' She jerked her spurs into the restless horse's sides. 'Stand still,' she commanded, 'or I'll have your arse!' She recovered herself quickly and smiled winningly at the General. 'Any time you are ready, *I am*.' The innuendo was obvious in her voice.

The General mopped his brow quickly and said to the Terrible Triplets, 'The things I do for France.' And then, 'Gentlemen, let us give it another hour and *then* we move . . .'

*

At that very moment some forty kilometres away, Jones, the HMS *Swordfish*'s sonar operator, fitted his headphones and turned up the speaker. Suddenly the compartment was flooded with *pings*.

Higgs called over to the radar operator, 'What's the range?'

Before he could answer, Jones said, 'High speed screws. Bearing zero-four-eight. Closing on our bow.'

'What do you make of her?' Higgs asked quickly

'Don't know, sir,' Jones answered his brow furrowed with concentration. 'But she's running low in the water.'

'Another sub. sir?' the bosun suggested.

Higgs did not answer. He was listening intently.

A moment later, Jones confirmed the bosun's identification. 'Yessir, it's another sub all right.'

Suddenly everything in the compartment was deadly silent, while the *pings* grew ever louder but alternated in tone at regular intervals.

'They're scanning still,' Higgs said to no one in particular. 'They haven't locked on to us yet.' Even as he said the words, he realized that his own forebodings had been realized. What would another submarine be doing off the French coast making a sonar search? Obviously. the Germans were making a routine search. Perhaps they did not expect to find a sub – a surface vessel was obviously more likely. But one thing was certain: they expected *somebody*. Somehow, their mission had been betrayed.

Five minutes later the enemy sub swept by the silent, motionless *Swordfish* by a matter of yards without having detected her but leaving her captain and crew shaken and ashen-faced. Each man asked himself one overwhelming question: *How were they ever going to get out of the bay again?*

Sitting on the balcony watching the General through field glasses, oblivious to the exultation of the crowd below as the first *course royale* commenced, Agnelli told himself that his mission was almost completed. Whatever game the General had prepared in his foolish attempt to get out of

Nîmes, he would never reach the coast – but if by some chance he managed it, the Tommies would never pick him up. Thanks to that fool Reynaud, everything was sealed up nice and tight.

The thought pleased him. As he lowered his glasses and started to concentrate on the hectic activity below, he promised himself a treat this night when this Gilles business was all over: a fine buxom virgin from the country.

THREE

'Will yer just get a load of that!' Matz breathed in awe, as the mass of girls came tripping gaily towards the road block, waving wine bottles. Their bodies swayed provocatively and their bodices were opened in wild abandon, revealing ample breasts, to the soldiers' delighted gaze.

'Pinch me and tell me I'm dreaming, Schulze. I don't know a fart from a flame-thrower any more!'

'Pinch you – I'll kick you!' Schulze roared, as the screaming, squealing girls swamped the barrier, thrusting their experienced bodies at the astonished young troopers, who flushed at such unexpected forwardness, completely overwhelmed at the sight of so much naked flesh.

'Like a whole bleedin' girls' school,' a delighted soldier roared and disappeared into the female mass.

'Get off!' Schulze bellowed, thrusting aside a dark-eyed girl with bold eyes and a carmen mouth, who pushed her pointed breasts under his nose, as if she were offering him them on a silver tray. 'What in hell do you think this is, eh? Ça suffi, cons.' His face grew scarlet with anger as he pushed the excited girls to one side and tried to rescue his overwhelmed little command. 'Get yer paws off my lads! Come on, knock it off! They're too young for that kind of thing!'

'Nix!' He slapped the skilled fingers of one of the girls, who was busy touching one very surprised trooper suggestively, as if she were testing the quality of a particular type of fruit. With his other hand he pulled back a blond boy whose face was buried deep between a girl's breasts. Suddenly Schulze caught sight of a familiar face. 'Hey, Marie,' he yelled, 'who let you out? This isn't your usual day –'

A clatter of hooves drowned the rest of his question. Schulze swung round and saw an enormous fat woman mounted on a horse that seemed about to give way in the middle at any moment. She was cracking her long whip frantically so that her tremendous breasts trembled like puddings underneath the tight blouse.

'Holy strawsack!' Matz gasped. 'Surely they have to pump her up every morning. She couldn't be *that* big!'

The next instant the two Germans sprang out of the way as two young bulls, their horns gleaming lethally in the hot sun, skidded round the corner, breathing fire from their distended nostrils. Schulze caught a frightening glimpse of a dark muzzle and angry red-rimmed eyes looking straight at him and quickly smashed through a near-by window. Just in time. The bull charged, ramming straight into the wall with an impact that Schulze, sprawled full-length in broken glass, could feel.

It was Matz's turn to flee as the second bull prepared to charge, its muscles quickening in excitement. He threw himself over the heap of sandbags which housed their machine-gun and cringed as the bull struck it with full force, showering him with sand so that he did not see the band of young men in immaculate white urging on the bulls, with '*Hah, hah, venga . . . toro . . . VENGA!*'

In an instant the road block was shattered, a confused mêlée of screaming women, shouting soldiers, yelling civilians and bellowing bulls.

Not everyone at the surprised barricade forgot his duty in that moment of chaos. Trooper Schneider, whose greatest ambition in life was to become a lance-corporal in the Regular SS, recognized the older civilian's face when it was almost too late. Hastily he unslung his machine-pistol and barred the sweating man's way. 'Hey, you, hold it!'

Surprisingly, the civilian with the large hooked nose understood German. As the others streamed forward through the shattered road block, he said, 'What is it, soldier?'

'I know your face – you're the general we're looking for,' Schneider growled. Suddenly he realized what this meant. It meant *tin*, and tin undoubtedly meant promotion.

Gilles glanced around him. The dust raised by the flying hooves obscured everything. For an instant the two men were alone in the fog. 'But I can prove I'm not a general. Why, I'm just a humble farmer.' He reached into his pocket and fumbled there, as if he were looking for his identity card.

Abruptly, steel flashed, a swinging right arc to the belly. The boy saw the movement, but he seemed paralysed. The blade disappeared into the cloth, right up to the hilt, causing Schneider to suck a noisy lungful of air in through his gaping mouth. Gilles plunged home the knife once more. Schneider sagged against him like a drunk and, looking up at him with dull, unseeing eyes, the life gone from him. Gilles looked at the youth, aghast. He looked at the German's light-blue eyes and fresh, bronzed cheeks: his life had been short and probably not very sweet. Then the deadweight of the body became too much for him. He let the German slump in the dust and began running after the others, with frightening suddenness, aware of his own frail mortality.

The dead boy lay between two pyramids of animal dung, which smoked like twin camp fires, a pair of abandoned lace panties lying incongruously at the base of his big nailed-studded boots.

'Why didn't you inform me at once, Schulze?' von Dodenburg asked, closing the dead boy's eyelids and then rising slowly to his feet.

'Because, sir, I thought at first he'd been hit by one of those shitting Frog bulls – or perhaps a horse. They were running around all over the show. Then I saw the knife sticking out of the poor sod's guts and I knew something funny had happened.'

'But what makes you think the French general we're looking for had anything to do with this?' Von Dodenburg raised his voice above the frenzied noise of the festival.

'Because Marie is one of the whores from the local brothel.'

'I don't understand, Schulze.'

'Well, sir, it stands to reason. I mean, tarts like that don't go faffing around with a lot of bulls.'

'Yer,' Matz chimed in. 'The only balls they see is on their back with their legs in the air.'

'I said *bulls*, you little ape-turd.'

'I know,' Matz persisted, 'balls!'

'Shut up,' von Dodenburg snapped, making up his mind. 'Signaller!'

The radio operator dropped smartly over the side of the command halftrack, its engine ready for instant action. 'Sir!'

'Take a message to the CO and all other companies.'

The signaller started to scribble swiftly on his pad.

'General Gilles broken through screen at southern exit road between Nîmes and Uchaud. Believe him to be heading for the sea. Could take either side road to Vauvert or the next one to Aimargues. Probable destination Le Grau du Roi. Suggest the Navy be alerted. First Company taking up chase.' He hesitated barely a moment, knowing that time was of the essence but knowing, too, that he was going to bring a storm down about his head by signing this message. 'Sign it,' he commanded, 'von Dodenburg. Clear?'

'Clear, sir.'

'All right, off with you. Send it.'

As the signaller doubled back to the halftrack, von Dodenburg turned to the crestfallen little section, who now realized that they had been cheated of the coveted decoration. 'All right, you bunch of bird-brains, you've made a damned mess of things. But, in three devils' name, you're going to put it right again. Or, by God, I'll have the lot of you doing fatigues until your tongues hang down to your bootlaces. Assuming this French general and his party are heading for the sea south of here, we've got to get there ahead of them. If they're warned and make a break for the Etang du Roi lake, we're in bad trouble. That place is a mess of reeds, little islands and hidden paths. We'd need a whole division to weed them out of there. All right, you layabouts, at the double. *Mount up!*'

Frantically, the chastened soldiers doubled for the half-track, whose driver was already gunning his engine, impatient to be off. One moment later they were clattering south at top speed.

The hunt was on!

FOUR

As planned, the makeshift group were beginning to scatter. The girls under Madame Broglie would head for Vauvert. The men with the bulls would attempt to cross country and lead a false trail to Albaron. The General knew it would be risky, especially now after he had killed the boy. He had no illusions about what the *SS* would do, even to the girls, if they caught them. He flashed a look at the sky: fortunately, the sun was beginning to go down. Within the next hour it would be completely dark. Hopefully the darkness would last long enough for them to make the coast and be picked up – then he remembered that a full moon was due later that night.

While the men with the bulls left the road and plunged into the marshy terrain the General and the three Englishmen changed into blue peasant working smocks and Basque berets, hastily concealing their weapons beneath the wide overalls. Then the General looked at Madame Broglie and offered his hand with unaccustomed formality. 'Madame, you have lost your house and livelihood because of us. I am sorry, but I thank you all the same.'

Madame Broglie, sitting astride the groaning nag, drew herself up proudly. 'I know,' she cried, her gold teeth glittering in the rays of the setting sun. 'But I do it for France.'

The General raised his right hand to his beret in salute and Madame Broglie returned the gesture, her massive bosom straining at her tight silk blouse so much that Tiddey-Oggy instinctively half-covered his face, as if he expected her buttons to pop off and hit him like bullets.

159

'And you, *mon Ge neral?*'

Gilles flashed the three Englishmen a warning look. 'We'll probably follow the coast up to the south of the *Etang de Mauguio*,' he lied glibly. 'It is a safe place to be picked up.'

'I see. Well, General, we must go.'

'You must.'

Madame Broglie forced the weary horse's head round and it started to plod back along the road, its hind legs spread outwards under her weight. Her girls began to follow. Some of them turned and waved their handkerchiefs, like convent girls returning to their cloistered halls after a day's outing; others wept openly.

'Till another and a better day, ladies,' General Gilles cried after them and then turned to the waiting Englishmen. 'I was forced to lie about our rendezvous to them, you understand. If they are caught – and, undoubtedly they will be – it is better that they do not know too much when the Gestapo starts questioning them. It is hard to mislead the people who have helped one so much. But it is the world in which we live,' he added, dismissing Madame Broglie and her whores. 'I shall now tell you our rendezvous. It is the coast just off the village of Le Grau du Roi.'

'It don't mean much to me,' Tiddey-Oggy commented grumpily.

'Natch,' Tonsils quipped. 'Nothing means much to you 'cept feeding your face with that bloody awful cornish pasty o' yourn.'

'But, of course, he's right,' the General interjected quickly. 'Why should it mean anything to you? But for our purposes, its position is excellent. To the rear it is protected from any interference by motorized German troops by the lake which is located there and the marshy ground to both south and north. This means that if the Germans were lucky enough to get a lead to our whereabouts, we have only the road – to the south or the north – to defend, and it is so narrow that the four of us could do it alone.'

'We've got to get there first,' Tiddey-Oggy grumbled.

'Never count your chickens before they're hatched, I always say.'

'Oh, shut up,' The Toff said.

'But, agreed, we have to get there first. We can't go cross country to Le Grau because of the marshes. But we must assume that the Boche will be watching the roads, so in following the road network, we will have to keep to the embankments which are firm, ready to hide if we spot a Boche patrol. Clear?'

They nodded their heads in unison. There was no doubt that General Gilles was a leader of men. He talked to them in the same manner as their ex-CO had done, and as expertly, as if everything were simple and under control.

'There is nothing to stop us on our route, save the bridge at Aigues Mortes.' He smiled suddenly, in spite of the danger and urgency of their position. 'But my faithful Pierre will take care of that.'

The Englishmen had been wondering what had happened to the silent batman.

'I sent him ahead early this morning, before dawn, foreseeing such an emergency. If the Boche are guarding the bridge, he is to secure a boat further up the river and ferry us across. Knowing the good Pierre as I do, I am confident that he will find a boat for money, or – ' He did not complete the sentence. Instead, he drew his forefinger under his throat in a slitting motion.

The Toff shuddered.

'All right, gentlemen, there is no time to be lost. From now it is to be, as we say in France, *marchez ou crevez* – march or die.'

'In the name of the devil!' The Vulture cursed and brought his riding crop down hard on the top of the staff car's radiator. 'Can nothing go right in this battalion!'

Sergeant-Major Metzger looked down at his feet. It was not wise to catch The Vulture's eye at the moment.

They were standing on the narrow elevated road that led

from the hamlet of St Laurent d'Aigouze to the sea. Darkness was already beginning to fall and a long column of vehicles stood stalled behind them as The Vulture attempted to decide what to do next, now that there was no further information coming in from von Dodenburg, who had seemingly vanished into the blue.

'If only I knew that we were not on a wild goose chase! How can that fool von Dodenburg presuppose that they are heading for this place, le Grau? There must be a half a hundred spots on this coast where the Frenchman could be picked up.'

Metzger continued to look at his boots.

The Vulture made up his mind. 'All right, Sergeant-Major, you'll take a section and secure the bridge at Aigues Mortes. If they're heading for the coast, they'll have to cross it. We'll scour the countryside in the meantime. Don't just stand there, Sergeant-Major, get your section together and make dust!'

'Sir!' Sergeant-Major Metzger replied with more enthusiasm than he felt.

The Butcher set up his guard-posts at both ends of the iron-frame bridge outside the already sleeping village and stared gloomily at the murky, slow-running water. It was going to be a long night.

FIVE

Pierre cursed in quiet desperation. He had searched the length of the river as far as he dared and had not found a boat anywhere, save here, one hundred metres away from the bridge. The Boche, however, had set up a guard-post virtually within spitting distance of where the rowing boat lay.

Pierre lay quietly in the thick darkness, wondering how he could pull it off. For a while he toyed with the idea of swimming down river to it, but he was not a good swimmer and the noise he would make would certainly alert the guards. Although the terrain leading down to the bank was marshy, he felt he would make less noise crawling there than he would swimming. Time was running out. The General would spot immediately that the bridge was guarded; then he would start searching the banks for him and the boat. It must be ready.

Carefully, Pierre stowed his treasured pipe in an inside pocket and then began to slither over the marshy ground towards the bank. Panting hard, he crawled nearer to his objective. On the bridge, the Boches' coal-scuttle helmets were clearly outlined against the growing silver. Another ten minutes, he told himself, and the whole countryside would be ablaze with moonlight. He forced himself to quicken his pace.

On the bridge Sergeant-Major Metzger decided he would shorten the tedium of the long guard by relieving himself. 'All right, you lot of weak-kneed wet-tails, I'm off on a mission.' He raised his right leg to knee height and gave an energetic fart. 'Keep your eyes skinned in the meantime.

Now who's got any arse paper in his pocket – and none of that emery-paper stuff the storehouse bulls dish out to you common soldiers. Come on, move it. Paper, I said!'

Metzger had just assumed a squatting position when he heard a strange, slithering noise which made him forget his needs for that night and indeed for several nights to come.

He grabbed for his dirk at the same moment that the mud-smeared civilian loomed up out of the darkness. With his trousers hanging foolishly around his ankles, Metzger lunged forward. Pierre, as startled as The Butcher, chopped his fist down on the Boche's wrist instinctively. The Butcher grunted with pain and let the dirk drop. Pierre smashed his fist into Metzger's face, sending him sprawling full-length, shirt-tail flapping around his naked buttocks. Pierre dived on top of him, determined to silence him before he could give a call for help.

Desperately, The Butcher tried to free himself from the grip around his throat. Blow upon blow he smashed into Pierre's face, but still he held on. The Butcher felt himself growing faint as stars started to explode in front of his eyes. Still Pierre did not relax his vice-like hold. Wildly, Metzger's outstretched fingers sought for the dirk he had dropped. He must find it soon or in a matter of seconds he would black out altogether. His fingers grasped its ivory handle. With the last of his strength he rammed its blade into the Frenchman's side. Pierre arched in agony; his screams rent the night air, alarming the guard on the bridge.

'*Mon General!*' Then, mouth gaping wide with the pain of death, Pierre fell down dead on top of the unconscious Butcher.

The bridge loomed out of the darkness like a prehistoric monster lumbering out of primeval slime at the instant that they heard the desperate warning. General Gilles under-stood at once. 'Pierre, it's Pierre!' he whispered urgently, holding them back. 'They've got him!'

The four men crouched hurriedly as the lights began to flash on the bridge. General Gilles bit his bottom lip. He knew they would not have taken his ex-batman alive: Pierre had sworn never again to be a captive of the Boche; his experiences in the camp in Upper Silesia during the first show had been enough for him.

Next to him, The Toff voiced his own unspoken question, 'What now, General?'

'It looks as if most of the guards have gone over to the other side on account of poor Pierre. At all events, their attention is distracted.' He rose to his feet. 'Come on,' he commanded urgently. 'To the bridge.'

'But we can't go over it,' Tiddey-Oggy protested.

'Of course not, but we can go *under* it. Follow me.'

Plop. There was a spurt of water on the dull-silver surface of the river. Gilles felt his heart beating like a trip hammer. What was the sudden noise which had caught them when they were already halfway across? Another *plop* broke the heavy silence. Suddenly, Tonsils pressed his mouth close to the General's ear and whispered, 'It's a Jerry right above us. He's throwing stones into the water.'

Gilles's heart leapt. Of course! He whispered a hoarse 'Come on' and they resumed their laborious climb underneath the bridge, swinging from girder to girder, clamping their legs around the next stanchion before letting go with their hands, then repeating the operation. There was not much of a drop, but they knew that if they fell it would mean death: the enemy would spot them at once.

Dripping with sweat, the General grunted and threw his legs out into space. He was very fit for a man of fifty, but the strain was telling. His boots slapped against the stanchion and his legs wrapped around it. He took a deep breath and let go. *His hands failed to connect!* In a flash he was hanging upside down, his leg muscles taking an almost unbearable strain.

Surprisingly, Tiddey-Oggy reacted first. 'Grab me sodding legs, Tonsils,' he grunted and dived forward, hands first, hardly waiting for the red-haired Cockney to take hold.

Suspended in mid-air, he sought and found the General's

hands. 'Listen!' he grunted through tightly clenched teeth, his leg muscles ablaze as he bore the weight of the General's body, too, now. 'I'm going to lift you up . . . But we've got . . . got to be quick. 'Now!'

Above them the girders rang with the steady noise of a guard's heavy boots. Tiddey-Oggy raised the General until his frantic fingers found a hold. Then he let go with one hand and grabbed for a girder himself. They rested for a few moments until the sound of heavy boots on the far end of the bridge indicated that the rest of the Germans were returning. Quickly, they resumed their laborious progress. Ten minutes later they were lying full-length in the mud of the other side, their breaths coming in short gasps and their limbs trembling violently from the exertion. But there was the light of triumph in their eyes. They had overcome the last barrier. They were going to make it.

'Seven more kilometres to the coast,' the General announced finally, rising to his feet.

'England, home and beauty, here we come,' Tonsils said exuberantly. 'Come on, me lucky lads, all aboard for the *Skylark*.'

Chuckling, the four men disappeared into the glowing darkness.

SIX

All was silent save for the soft, sad *lap-lap* of the waves at the beach below and the hoarse cry of some night bird in the marshes which bordered the lake. The moon was beginning to bathe the sea in a shimmering light.

Pressed together on the embankment which bordered the narrow coastal road, the four men searched the water for the green signal light which would indicate that the submarine was in position. More than once they saw lights flashing out to sea answered by other lights along the coast. Perhaps, the General concluded, chilled a little by the breeze from the sea, it was the Boche signalling to one another. Sea patrols probably.

Just when they were beginning to despair that they would ever spot the signal, it came – four short spurts of green.

'It's them!' Tonsils cried excitedly. '*The sub!*'

'Come on, gentlemen,' General Gilles said happily. 'We must not keep your compatriots waiting. Let us proceed to the beach.'

'Yer,' Tonsils agreed, 'what are we waiting for, mates, let's go.'

They ploughed through the damp sand, their weariness forgotten now, spurred on by the thought that soon they would be on their way to England.

'The dinghy, I think I can hear the dinghy!' The Toff said, turning his head into the wind and stopping to hear better. 'It's over there, to our right.'

Gilles stopped, too. For a moment he heard nothing, then the soft, careful swish of oars; whoever was propelling the unseen craft was being very careful, anticipating a sudden challenge and possible disaster.

'You're right. Over there. It sounds like the dinghy. Come on – quick!'

Changing direction, they began to plod on towards the sound of the oars. Tonsils whistled *South of the Border – Down Mexico Way* through his teeth in happy anticipation.

With dramatic suddenness, the spotlight on von Dodenburg's halftrack, positioned above the road, cut the silver gloom. The white light swung round, feeling the darkness, seeking them with frightening certainty.

'*Stehenbleiben!*' a harsh voice ordered loudly. '*Stehenbleiben – oder wir schiessen!*'*

'*Boche!*' General Gilles gasped.

Tonsils raised the captured Schmeisser and fired a violent burst at the searchlight. There was the sound of smashing glass, a scream of pain, a curse. Abruptly the light went out.

'Run for it!' Gilles yelled.

Behind them there were angry shouts and the sound of a motor starting up. Heavy nailed boots clattered across the road. A machine-gun opened fire. White tracer curved over their heads, gathering speed at every moment, zipping out across the sea towards the dinghy. The Germans had spotted it, too!

The Toff, pelting along with the rest through the deep, damp sand, knew they were not going to make it. By the time the dinghy anchored on the beach and they boarded it, the Germans would be upon them. He made his decision: 'Chaps, there's no use, I'm staying behind.' Dropping on to the sand, he fired an angry volley at the advancing Germans. At once the heavy machine-gun turned its fire in his direction. Tracer started to wing its way towards him like a flight of angry hornets.

First Tiddey-Oggy, then Tonsils stopped.

The General ran on; only when he realized the Englishmen were not with him did he stop too. 'What is it?' he breathed.

* Stop or we'll shoot.

'Yer?' the other two demanded.

'Keep on going. I'll cover you. You won't make it otherwise.' The Toff fired another burst in the direction of the machine-gun and was rewarded by screams of pain and then silence as the machine-gun stopped firing. 'It's the only way to save the General – '

Tonsils looked at Tiddey-Oggy in the red gloom. Then they too dropped into the sand and began firing.

'Go on, sir!' Tiddey-Oggy urged, the machine-pistol quivering in his capable hands. 'Three ordinary squaddies like us won't be missed much. But you're a general,' he grunted with the effort of firing; 'you're important.'

'Give my love to the Big Smoke, sir!' Tonsils yelled without turning round, firing a furious burst at the suddenly stalled German infantry.

General Gilles hesitated. His first instinct was to drop down with them in the sand and die like the soldier he had been all his life. Hadn't he often told himself in moments of utter honesty that he wanted to die on the battlefield and not in bed? Then he thought of France – France was more important than human life. 'Gentlemen, I thank you. You will not be forgotten.' He turned, his eyes flooding with tears, and began to run towards the sound of the oars.

Von Dodenburg made his dispositions quickly. 'Spread out on both flanks!' he yelled above the chatter of machine-pistol fire which was keeping his men bogged down in the sand. 'At the double! You here in the centre, give us covering fire. *At the double now!* Matz and Schulze, with me!'

Crouched low, followed by the others, he doubled back to the bullet-pocked halftrack with its driver slumped dead over the wheel and its deck packed with badly wounded grenadiers. Hastily, he prised open the lid of a box of grenades and stuffed half a dozen stick grenades in his belt. Matz and Schulze followed suit without orders, knowing instinctively what the CO was intending to do.

*

The Toff was hit first, when a grenade exploded in a ball of angry purple a couple of yards in front of him. He reeled back, his face bloodied. Tonsils dropped his Schmeisser and tried to grab him as he writhed in the sand in agony, but The Toff pushed him away. 'Sorry,' he said apologetically. 'I'm afraid I've bought it . . .'

'*The sods, the fucking sods!*' Tonsils sobbed, staggering to his feet and running blindly towards the Germans with the bombs, firing wildly from the hip. 'Come on, let's see how you can fight now!'

'Great crap on the Christmas tree!' Schulze roared in awe as the slim young figure in the tattered smock staggered towards him. 'Now I know the Tommies are shitting crazy!' He pulled the china pin at the base of the stick grenade and lobbed it easily, directly in his path.

Tonsils disappeared in a great searing flame, cursing with Cockney fluency until von Dodenburg, taking pity on the blinded, legless piece of human misery writhing on the sand at his feet, bent down and placed the muzzle of his pistol at the back of the Tommy's skull almost tenderly and pressed the trigger, shattering it into a thousand pieces.

Tiddey-Oggy held them back another five minutes, until three grenades exploded right on top of him. All they ever found of him afterwards was his boots.

SEVEN

The general was dragged on to the wet deck. 'Higgs,' the young skipper said, introducing himself quickly.

'Gilles.' The General attempted to make a bow, but Higgs did not give him time.

'We've got to get below – *at once*, sir!'

In the conning tower the Lewis gun was already beginning to chatter, sending an urgent stream of tracer to the shore. All along the coast, searchlights were flicking on. Scarlet flame stabbed the night, and from somewhere in the dark night there came the howl of racing engines. E-boats, Higgs told himself instinctively as he doubled after the General along the wet, narrow deck.

The searchlights on the shore tried to find them, crisscrossing each other's path, forming boxes which were parted by icy white fingers until they were found to be empty. In a matter of minutes, Higgs knew they would find *Swordfish* and then the artillery would open up.

He fastened the hatch catches with tembling fingers and hushed down the steel pole. Inside all was in order. He flung one last glance around the green-glowing compartment. 'All right, take her down.'

The bosun looked at him, aghast.

'I know . . . I know,' he answered the man's unspoken question angrily. 'I know it's too bloody shallow! But what else are we to do? I can't chance fighting it out with E-boats and artillery on the surface. Let's go!'

There was a rush of escaping compressed air as their tanks started to flood. Higgs had no time for niceties now. The boat was going down at a terrible angle. But the *pings* from the sonar were getting louder and louder. It would only be a matter of minutes and then the E-boats would be directly above them. At a forty degree angle, the *Swordfish* hit bottom with a nasty bump that set everybody grabbing for support.

'Make your depth thirty feet,' Higgs commanded.

'Thirty feet it is, sir!' the reply came back hurriedly. The *pings* were getting ever louder.

'Shut negative flood! Blow negative to the mark!' His order was carried out. He rang the engine control and gave his order.

'Engines secured! Ahead one third!'

Colour returned to the seamen's tense faces as the submarine started to move ahead. The bump had not injured the *Swordfish*. She was moving forward without a drop of water having penetrated her fabric.

The *pings* were almost on top of them now. The General, only half-understanding what was going on, flashed a worried look from face to face. The crew, knowing what must come soon, avoided his gaze; they had other things to do than help this elderly, shabby civilian overcome his bewilderment and fear.

Higgs knew there was no trying to sit it out in the bay. The E-boats would cover the area back and forth with their depth charges until they found him. He had to attempt to make a run for it and hope for the best. 'Silent running,' he ordered. A little voice within him said cynically, 'And you'd better well bloody pray, too!'

'Picking up splashes,' the sonar operator reported, his voice tense. 'Depth charges coming down, sir!'

There was the sound of racing engines directly above them, then a click as the charge armed. The blast wave rocked the submarine from side to side, as if it were a toy, flinging the seamen to the deck.

A second charge followed. It was very close. Trembling, Higgs wondered how the E-boat could miss in such shallow water. It exploded with a tremendous blast, shattering light bulbs. Paint chips tumbled from the steel walls in a grey rain. In the galley the plates came rattling down. Here and there a metal seam gave and water started to trickle in.

Higgs found his voice in spite of the petrifying shock of the blast. 'Get on to those leaks, lads!' he ordered. 'At the double, now!'

Then the roaring screws passed and all was silent, save for the noise made by the men with hammers as they rammed home the patches.

The sonar operator spoke again. 'High speed screws approaching, sir . . . starboard ninety degrees angle . . .another E-boat!'

'All engines stop!' Higgs ordered, hoping that the manoeuvre would fool the Germans.

'Picking up splashes,' the operator reported. 'Charges coming down again, sir!'

Once, twice, three times! HMS *Swordfish* shuddered under the cruel blows. Plates gave. Higgs thought he heard a chain snap in the forward torpedo room. Water started to pour in everywhere. The boat could not withstand much more of this.

Higgs stared at the General, green and sick with fear, then looked at his men, their faces ashen as the boat was racked yet again with violent spasms. He knew he must do something – and do it soon! Suddenly it came to him. The E-boats were only armed with torpedoes and light machine-guns. He had a three-inch gun on deck. If he could bull his way through them on the surface until he reached the open sea . . . He did not wait to think the thought out. It was their last chance. '*Gun crew!*' he yelled above the ear-shattering explosions. 'Stand by to surface! All right,' he snarled at the surprised bosun, 'get ready to take her up. And I want the machine-gunners on that tower with me. At the double!'

'*All right, take her up!*'

With dramatic suddenness, HMS *Swordfish* surfaced in the swirling water. Even before the E-boats' searchlights swerved round and pinned her down in their blinding light, the gun crew under the bosun's command raced madly down the wet deck towards the three-inch deck gun, while the Lewis gunners grabbed their weapons and, smacking on a round pan of ammunition, began to spit angry red tracer at the closest E-boat.

The sub swung round and came racing in at thirty-five knots, bow slicing the water as if it were hitting a series of brick walls. First one, then the other of the two torpedoes she carried thudded into the water in the same instant that the flying wooden boat broke to one side, the Lewis gunners ripping huge chunks out of her superstructure.

Higgs had no time to consider the damage he was inflicting upon the enemy. 'Hard to port!' he bellowed, as the trail of white bubbles, clearly visible in the moonlight, came rushing towards the *Swordfish* at an alarming rate. Higgs said a quick prayer that the helmsman would react quickly enough.

The two torpedoes hissed by with only feet to spare.

The second E-boat came speeding in with a banshee howl from its tremendous engines, two white wings of water flying up high at its stern almost obscuring it.

The bosun was not put off by the smallness and speed of the target. '*Fire!*' he cried when the E-boat was less than two hundred yards away.

The deck gun erupted. Vicious scarlet flame stabbed the darkness. The speeding E-boat came to a dead stop. Nothing seemed to have happened.

'*Fire!*' the furious bosun cried. 'Knock the bastard – '

His words were drowned in a thunderous explosion. A blinding blue flame seared into the darkness. The E-boat was lifted bodily out of the water and came smashing down again in flames.

'*Hurrah!*' cheered the gun crew, and the men on the conning tower yelled in hoarse triumph.

Higgs knew there was no time for self-congratulations. Other E-boats were speeding in on them, twisting and turning violently, throwing up huge wakes of wild white water as they attempted to throw the submarine's gunners off.

Higgs heard the General cry '*Torpedoes!*' just in time. Taking advantage of the main E-boat attack, another lone torpedo-boat had sneaked in from the rear and launched its fish unnoticed.

'Hard to starboard,' Higgs yelled urgently. 'For Chrissake, move it! *Hard* – '

The words died on his lips as the torpedoes, easily identifiable by their bubbling white wake, came hissing straight towards the *Swordfish*. Would the helmsman manage to bring the boat round in time?

Higgs tensed for the blow that must come. Both fish rushed by the churning wake of the submarine, heading straight into the red and white maelstrom of flying steel and angry red tracer that came from the E-boat pack. The leading E-boat heeled violently as the first fish struck it. A second later it exploded in a tremendous flash of violet light.

'They've had enough! *They've sodding well had enough!*' someone behind Higgs cried excitedly. '*They're buggering off!*'

Higgs could hardly believe the evidence of his own eyes. The E-boats were swinging around in great flying white curves, followed by the splashes of the *Swordfish*'s shells exploding, and racing for cover.

'*Nom de Dieu!*' General Gilles cried enthusiastically. 'Captain, we've done it. The way ahead is clear!'

On the height overlooking the exit from the bay, The Vulture lashed his cane against the backs of his tank crews as they raced for their Mark IIIs. 'Run, you dogs of death!' he rasped, chasing behind them like a sheep-dog, slashing about him. 'If you don't get there in time, I'll have – '

There was no need to conclude his usual threat. His panting tankers were already clambering up on to their tanks, diving into their turrets, clicking on switches with shaking fingers, pulling on their headsets, grabbing the gleaming forty-kilo shells out of the racks – automatically carrying out the hundred and one little actions needed to fire their cannon.

'*Headlights on!*' The Vulture commanded, running from one tank to another and ripping off the black-out covers.

The drivers flicked on their headlights. Below the bay was lit up with dramatic suddenness. Hastily, the gunners swung their turrets round to face the direction from which the noise of the sub's engines was coming, growing steadily louder by the minute.

The Vulture, his voice thick with tension, 'And don't you dare fail me, you gunners, or you'll wish that you'd never been born!'

The bosun was the first to spot the harsh yellow beams barring their way. 'Coastal – '

His words were drowned by a low roll, like distant thunder. On the headland to their right the night sky was ripped apart suddenly and a salvo of six shells plummeted out of the sky directly in front of the *Swordfish*.

The submarine heeled violently, throwing the seamen all about the conning tower. As Higgs grabbed a hold just in time, he caught a glimpse of General Gilles, bleeding as he lay in the corner.

The tank gunners fired again. With the sound of canvas being ripped apart violently, the monstrous salvo straddled the submarine. Shrapnel rapped at the conning tower, and on deck the gunners were strewn everywhere, in a tangled mess of men and metal.

'*Dive – take her down!*' Higgs bellowed frantically, while the sweating helmsman zig-zagged crazily, trying to throw off those yellow lights which continued to pin the submarine down.

The guns crashed into action once more. Red-hot, fist-sized shrapnel hissed into the conning tower. Higgs yelped with sudden agony as a piece bit into his right shoulder. Next to him a seaman dropped to the deck, minus his head, which rolled slowly into the scuppers like an abandoned football.

Weakly Higgs staggered to the hatch, followed by General Gilles, who was bleeding heavily from a head wound. He took hold of the tube and tried to slide down, but the pain in his shoulder was too intense, forcing him to let go. He fell heavily on to the dead body of Jones, whose head was still attached to the buzzing earphones. For a moment the skipper lay collapsed, while the deck plates heaved and strained from the battering the *Swordfish* was taking from the shells, each fresh salvo sending another cruel spasm shuddering through the submarine.

With an effort of will but green and sick with fear, Higgs staggered through dead men who lay everywhere in the shattered compartment. He sloshed through the dark, flooded hold trying to find out why his order to submerge had not been obeyed. The *Swordfish* was tilting badly to port in spite of all the efforts of the seamen, whose muscles bulged as they tried to right her. He staggered through a hatch. The engine-room was a shambles. The artificers were all dead, their greasy white overalls now crimson. At the telegraph, the grizzled ancient CPO hung on, obviously dying, a great ragged hole gaping in his skinny back.

'Chief,' Higgs gasped, up to his thighs in water as he waded across to the Scot, 'how are you?'

'Na so canny, sir,' he gasped when Higgs took him in his arms. Then his eyes rolled upwards and he was dead.

Higgs sobbed. There was no hope for HMS *Swordfish* now.

As the last of the lights flickered out, there were screams and splashes in the darkness.

'Don't panic, men!' Higgs yelled at the top of his voice. 'Abandon ship. *Don't panic!*' His own voice died in a cry of sudden fear as the water came pouring in. Now he was fighting for his own life, clawing and fighting his crew and the mad deluge of equipment and instruments that were carrying them towards the hatch, from which there was no escape. HMS *Swordfish* was sinking.

Gilles gasped and spluttered to stay afloat. He half-swallowed sea water and then spewed it out, choking and gasping for air. Behind him he heard a terrifying growl. He swung round, treading water, while the shells continued to whizz by overhead.

HMS *Swordfish* had up-ended herself. As her stern rose out of the water, her screws still churned purposelessly. The metal of her fabric creaked and howled in an almost human roar: it was the roar of death. For a moment the submarine was silhouetted a harsh black against the burning sky; an instant later, she hissed and sank to her grave.

Gilles was alone now, save the debris and the dead of the gun crew nudging back and forth in the waves that the shells had created. For a moment he stared at the crimson glare above the headland. It seemed as if France herself were afire. His dream of glory was over. He could never save France now. Gently he thrust away the bosun, whose dead body kept nudging him and pulled the plug from his life jacket.

General Gilles took one final look at his burning homeland and then turned and began to swim powerfully and purposefully out to sea.

The body of General Gilles was never found. The liberation of France four years later had been left to Symbole, planning and plotting in an obscure hotel in London. Gilles himself became a footnote in the official French history of World War Two: *General of the Army Gilles, 1888–1940, disappeared in the confused, purposeless fighting in the last stages of the 1940 Campaign.*

It was the only obituary that General de Gaulle would allow. He had a long memory.

The Terrible Triplets – The Toff, Tiddey-Oggy, Tonsils – together with the bodies of the dead submarine guncrew, which the men of *Wotan* had fished out of the water, were flung carelessly in a mass grave (There were many mass graves that year) in a forgotten corner in one of Nîmes' older cemeteries. It was marked simply by a wooden plaque bearing the legend: *Seven Unknown British Soldiers, Killed in Action, 1940.*

For a few years after the war, while the fervour of the Liberation had still not abated, pretty little French girls in neat aprons and white socks placed fresh flowers on the grave at regular intervals and said a silent prayer for the dead. But during the French building boom of the early 1960s, a leading local building contractor and highly respected citizen gave the building inspector a substantial bribe to look the other way while he cleared the cemetery in an unorthodox but time-saving way. Working by spotlights at night, two bulldozers ground over the tombs, throwing up skeletons and bones in hurried confusion, to be covered over again early next morning by the first layer of liquid concrete poured for the foundations of a multi-million-franc project.

The name of that building contractor and respected citizen? None other than Monsieur Agnelli . . .

Epilogue

'Do you know Matzi, I think it's about time that shitting *Wotan* went back to the war. This shitting peacetime stuff is killing me.'

Corporal Schulze,   August 1940

'Well, here it is!' The Vulture rasped, screwing his monocle into his eye more tightly and draining his champagne with excitement. 'From the All Highest, the Greatest Captain of All Time personally.'

This morning, however, the great news took the edge off his usual cynicism when he referred to Adolf Hitler. He handed von Dodenburg the special *Blitz*.* 'Here, my dear young friend, read it aloud. I'd like someone to say the words. They are music to my ears.' He grinned wolfishly at the morose Captain.

Reluctantly, von Dodenburg began to read:

Congratulations! Splendid achievement. Death of Gilles severe blow for British Empire. Please address my best wishes and congratulations to your excellent battalion.

With German Greeting

In spite of his depression, von Dodenburg's heart leapt. The signal was signed *Adolf Hitler*.

'Yes, from the Führer himself!' The Vulture exclaimed delightedly. 'Beautiful music, what? *Major* Geier will soon be *Colonel* Geier. Even those base stallions in Berlin will have got the word by now. *Geier must be promoted!*' The Vulture filled a glass for von Dodenburg, then refilled his own. '*Prost!*'

'*Prost!*' von Dodenburg replied, his heart not in it.

Outside the mistral howled. The July sky was dark and overcast, and somewhere in the barracks a door was creaking

* An urgent military message.

on rusty springs in the wind, as if the place was already long abandoned. Von Dodenburg felt miserable.

The Vulture drained his glass, noticing that the Captain had hardly touched his. 'What's the matter, von Dodenburg? Why so gloomy on a splendid day like this?'

'It's that business with the submarine, sir. It's got out. The civilian populace know about it. I drove through the old city this morning just after breakfast and I could almost feel their resentment and hatred.' He shuddered and added, 'A louse just ran over my liver.'

The Vulture's smile did not vanish. 'But, my boy, that is typical post-festival depression, believe me. A combination of a hang-over and a bad conscience about the money they've spent and the women they've had.' He laughed happily and struck von Dodenburg a friendly blow on the shoulder. 'Nothing to worry about.'

A sudden squall of rain rattled the office window. The raindrops running down the pane like cold, bitter tears seemed to strengthen von Dodenburg's black mood. He shook his head firmly. 'I don't agree, sir. They are in a definitely anti-German mood. A couple of my chaps were attacked last night in the city by rowdies, and someone has been smearing anti-German slogans on the arena. I had the local French police remove them yesterday. That sinking of the sub has obviously stiffened their attitude to us.'

The Vulture shrugged carelessly. 'So? What does it matter? The Frogs are beaten. They are yesterday's problem, as far as I am concerned. Besides we are to evacuate the whole of southern France soon, as you know. Let their new leader, Marshal Petain, worry about the problem of Nîmes.' He leaned forward, his eyes sparkling and his voice low and confidential. 'A little canary at High Command – a fellow student at the War Academy just before the war – began to sing to me yesterday over a couple of bottles of champagne.'

'Sing?'

'Yes, and a pretty little tune it was,' The Vulture answered, still in a good mood. 'We are to move out ahead of the division. We are being transferred to the channel coast next week.'

Von Dodenburg's heart skipped a beat. 'You mean England? We are going to invade England?'

The Vulture tapped the side of his nose. 'Wooden eye, be on your guard,' he said sagely.

'I don't understand, sir,' von Dodenburg said, puzzled.

'My little canary from the High Command sang England. But I think, from other things he let drop, that the real invitation to the waltz will take place further east, much further east.'

Von Dodenburg looked at his CO in bewilderment. '*The east?*' he whispered, his brow furrowed.

'Yes. *Russia!*' His voice grew loud with enthusiasm. 'Think of it, von Dodenburg, all that territory to be conquered and the largest army in the world to be beaten. My God, your Hitler will call it a crusade.' He mimicked Hitler's thick Upper Austrian voice. ' "Let us not forget. We are not a spear thrown haphazardly into space, which may or may not find a target. We are the sword of the New Germany, wielded by the best hands and when called upon always ready to cut and thrust until our enemies are completely destroyed." You know how he rants on, von Dodenburg. Let him call it what he will, but I call it the best chance of being promoted for regular officers like ourselves there'll ever be in the whole of the twentieth century. My God,' he exclaimed, as if he had only just become aware of the magnitude of the operation himself, 'with a bit of luck I could be a general before I'm forty and, if those stinking red Ivans have any fight in them and the campaign goes on long enough, a field-marshal by the time I'm forty-five! The possibilities are boundless, my dear young friend.' Excitedly he filled their glasses with the last of the champagne. He squared his shoulders and raised his glass proudly, unable to know that he would be dead long before he reached the age of forty-five.* 'Let us drink a toast to Soviet Russia,' he rasped.

Von Dodenburg clicked to attention. He raised his glass level with the third button of his tunic, elbow extended at a right angle in the Prussian fashion, and waited for The

* See *Guns at Cassino* for further details.

Vulture's command.

'To Soviet Russia, von Dodenburg, and no heel taps! *Prost!*' The Vulture barked, his eyes sparkling with barely repressed excitement.

Von Dodenburg hesitated for a fraction of a second: he had a terrible vision of an interminable, treeless, icy waste, littered with the frozen bodies of the field-greys, and here and there a ragged, broken, crazed soldier fleeing back westwards before the sabres of the triumphant Cossacks. Then he, too, barked, 'To Soviet Russia! *Prost!*'

Draining their glasses, they shattered them against the office wall in a gesture of finality.

The die had been cast.

The leave truck bearing Schulze's squad squealed to a stop on the gleaming wet cobbles. Wearily the young troopers, their bones stiff from the long journey back from Paris and their heads still heavy from the bars and brothels, dropped over the tailgate and picked up their packs. Matz and Schulze, however, fell drunkenly from the truck, stinking of perfume and drink, singing *It don't mean a thing if you don't pull the string*, pulling imaginary lavatory chains as they did so, to be faced by a grim Sergeant-Major Metzger.

'Blue you are, you dogs! *BLUE!*' he bellowed at them, his face crimson.

'As full as a howitzer,' Matz chortled happily, wiping the raindrops that streamed down his wizened face with a pair of black lace panties he had stolen from the last Parisian whore he had slept with.

'Nissed as a pewt!' Schulze agreed, swaying dangerously from side to side. 'Nissed as a pewt!'

'Horrible banana-suckers!' The Butcher exploded, his eyes bulging out of his head at the sight of these two drunks on *his* square.

'Horrible banana-suckers we are, Sergeant-Major,' they both agreed happily.

Schulze stuck a big finger, covered with a fresh contraceptive, into his ear and dug up the wax. 'Can't be too

186

careful, Sergeant-Major,' he said thickly, boring into his ear as if he were trying to poke his finger right through his head. 'Germs everywhere, and my mother always told me to be very careful about germs.'

'Your mother can go and – '

'Naughty, naughty, dear Sergeant-Major,' the big Hamburger interrupted, wagging his other forefinger under the enraged NCO's nose. 'Mustn't say nasty words like that about dear mothers, dear old Metzger. After all, even sergeant-majors have mothers, don't they? Lord Jesus won't love you, you know . . . Come on, give us a kiss and say we are friends.' Schulze closed his eyes and puckered up his mouth expectantly.

Metzger drew out his silver whistle and blew three furious blasts on it. 'Turn out the guard!' he bellowed, beside himself with rage. 'For God's sake, turn out the guard and get these madmen off my back before I . . .' He spluttered, unable to finish the sentence, showering them with the foam from his lips.

'Look, it's snowing now,' Matz said mildly, wiping the liquid off his face.

'Funny summer we're having,' Schulze answered, just missing falling into the brightly polished fire-bucket at the last moment, apparently unaware of the heavy boots doubling across the square from the guardroom.

'Arrest them!' Metzger stuttered as the panting guard commander came to a halt in front of the turkey-red NCO. 'Arrest them and put 'em inside . . .'

'For how long, sir,' the frightened young corporal asked as he eyed Schulze, whose fearsome reputation was well-known within *Wotan*.

'For . . . *for ever!*' Metzger finally got the words out. 'Till hell freezes over, as far as I'm concerned. Just get the bastards out of my sight!'

The corporal nodded to his equally frightened squad. Hesitantly, they closed in on the two swaying, innanely grinning drunks, their rifles at the ready.

For once, Schulze did not live up to his reputation as the best bar-room brawler in the battalion. Tamely he and his running-mate let themselves be led off to the guard-room, passing an amused von Dodenburg, who had caught the end of their drunken conversation just before they disappeared inside.

'Do you know, Matzi,' said Schulze, 'I think it's about time that the shitting *Wotan* went back to the war. This shitting peacetime stuff is killing me . . .'

Silently, von Dodenburg nodded his head as if in agreement. Soon the trumpets would blare, the drums roll, the harsh commands echo and they would march once more. One thousand men. The élite of the élite. Young Germany – the black-uniformed conquerors of the West. This time they would march eastwards, embarking on an impossible adventure.

Sighing, Captain Kuno von Dodenburg turned and strode briskly into the bitter rain. *SS Assault Battalion Wotan* was returning to war . . .

All Futura Books are available at your bookshop or
newsagent, or can be ordered from the following
address:
Futura Books, Cash Sales Department,
P.O. Box 11, Falmouth, Cornwall.

Please send cheque or postal order (no currency), and
allow 25p for postage and packing for the first book
plus 10p per copy for each additional book ordered up to
a maximum charge of 95p in U.K.

Customers in Eire and B.F.P.O. please allow 25p for
postage and packing for the first book plus 10p per copy
for the next six books, thereafter 4p per book.

Overseas customers please allow 30p for postage and
packing for the first book and 10p per copy for each
additional book.